WHODUNIT ANTIQUES

BOOK 3: AN AUTOMATED MURDER

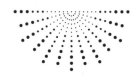

SHELLY WEST

CHAPTER ONE

Abigail Lane's gloved hands curled tightly around the cold rungs of the metal ladder. Her breath came out in jerky puffs of vapor, winding around the tiny icicles that hung from the gutter in front of her face.

She was now eye level with the front porch awning of Whodunit Antiques. The coil of Christmas lights braced over her arm threatened to send her tumbling off the ladder at any moment.

That was how she felt, at least. She could see, by peeking briefly down, that tumbling off the ladder would only mean a drop of four or five feet to the parking lot.

"Congratulations, dear," Grandma said dryly from her post at the base of the ladder. "You've made it to the fourth rung."

"I can't believe you've been hanging your own Christmas

lights all these years, Grandma," Abigail squeaked. She cleared her throat. "Do you know how dangerous this is?"

Grandma shrugged her shoulders. "All of these modern fears of heights and germs and safety hazards…" She shook her head in disbelief. "Back in my day, you'd let yourself get the occasional illness and broken bone. And you know what? You'd come out of it stronger than before!"

Abigail's vision blurred. Gritting her teeth, she forced herself to take another step up the ladder. "I'd happily go the rest of my life without breaking a bone, Grandma. Call me crazy."

"You *are* crazy," Grandma crowed from the comfort of solid ground. "You're terrified of heights and yet you insist on climbing up the ladder. I told you *I* could do it!"

"What I'm going through right now is far less terrifying than the thought of you climbing up this ladder."

With a sigh, Abigail maneuvered the lights onto the roof. She knew that, given half the chance, Grandma would be at the tippy-top of the ladder, teaching Abigail the proper way to hang lights. Though Grandma claimed frailty when socially convenient, the little old lady with the pure white braids piled atop her head was far from fragile.

Still, Abigail couldn't sit by and watch her grandmother risk her neck for the sake of a few lights. She waited too long to find out she even *had* a grandmother; she wasn't about to miss out on any more opportunities to help her.

For a few precious minutes, Abigail was able to focus. Grandma's store, Whodunit Antiques, occupied the bottom floor of a beautiful Victorian home. Normally, Abigail enjoyed the wooden framing of the three-story house. Today, however, she was pretty sure the original architects had overdone it.

"Oh!" Grandma suddenly gasped.

Startled, Abigail whipped around to look down at Grandma, the movement leaning the ladder precariously to her left. Just when she was sure the whole thing would topple sideways, Grandma noticed and yanked the ladder back to level.

"Well, don't get all flustered," Grandma said with a laugh. "It's just that James is jogging our way. He does look strapping, though, doesn't he?"

James, tall and dark, frumpily dressed yet dignified in posture, trotted up the sidewalk and came to a pause at the front of the store.

"Ladies," he said in greeting, running in place. His unruly curls spilled into his eyes as he peered up at Abigail. "You don't seem very comfortable up there, Cupcake. Need a hand?"

Abigail pried one arm and then the other loose from their death grip around the ladder frame. Straightening her shoulders, she continued stringing the lights as confidently as she could. "I'm doing just fine, thank you. Nice morning for a run."

James nodded. "Yeah, nice and cold."

"Tell me about it. I'm basically a popsicle by the time Thor and I finish up our morning runs." Abigail was proud of how even and utterly unafraid-of-heights her voice sounded. James, on the other hand, didn't seem convinced as he tilted his head up at her.

"Have you been running more, James?" Grandma asked. "I feel as if I've seen you often lately."

"I am," he answered, still jogging in place. "I've made more of a habit of it in the past month or so. It's great exercise, of course—gets me out of the motel. But it's also a great way to keep an eye on the goings-on around town."

"Have you sighted anything interesting?"

"Not lately, which is just the way I like it. Anyway, I was just stopping by to ask if you two have plans this evening."

"We can always make time," Grandma began. "Why? Do you have something in mind?"

"You know how the toy store downtown has been closed the past couple of weeks?"

Grandma nodded.

"Well, Mr. Yamamoto is having his grand winter reopening later today. He's renovated the place and has a new line of automata to unveil."

Grandma gasped. "I'm so glad you said something! It completely slipped my mind. I love Mr. Yamamoto's little creations. Do you know that I have one of his earlier automata? He made it as a child. It's this darling little squirrel nutcracker. It doesn't even require any muscle to use. You just wind it up and *crack* goes the nut!"

James stopped jogging in place as he smiled brightly. "I get the feeling he's got something really fascinating to reveal this winter. He's always upping his game. I remember begging my parents to stop at his store, even if it was just to look. I think it'd be a nice trip down memory lane to visit again."

"It certainly would be," Grandma agreed.

"Would you two like to meet me there? I'm dragging my father with me too, as much as Dad thinks it's silly."

"Willy will be there too?" Grandma shot a sly smile at Abigail. "I think it's a date then, isn't it, Abigail?"

Abigail twisted, trying to respond to Grandma's smile with a stern glare, but her vision blurred again. The ground seemed to drop farther away, and her stomach heaved.

"Yeah, sure," she said weakly, gulping cold air like a fish out of water. She hoped an affirmative answer would put an end to the entire conversation and send James off before he saw her have a panic attack.

James squinted up at her, then shook his head. "Okay. You be careful up there, Cupcake. It's a long fall." Grinning at Grandma, he gave them both a lazy salute and jogged away.

"You can come down now, Abigail," Grandma called as soon as James disappeared from view. "He's gone."

"I wasn't waiting for him to leave," Abigail protested, though she knew Grandma saw right through her bluff. Shakily, she reached down with one foot until it found the next rung, then she reached down with the next foot, and so on, until she finally touched dirt and leaves.

Grateful, she pushed away from the ladder and plopped

down. "Grandma, let's leave the lights up year-round so I never have to do that again."

Grandma laughed. "I won't make any promises, but I'll consider it. It does make me sad every time I have to take them down."

A streak of creamy fuzz shot off the porch and onto Abigail's lap. "Whoa, Missy, calm down," Abigail said, stroking the Shih Tzu's little head. The little dog, once plump and slow, had started joining Abigail on her own morning runs. Now, Missy was sleek, swift, and surprisingly strong. To her disappointment, however, Thor, her fellow dog companion, hardly seemed to notice the improvement in her figure.

"Yeah, you thought I was gonna fall, didn't you, girl?" Abigail scratched Missy behind the ears and looked around for her tan Great Dane. She found Thor at the far end of the porch, his head hanging off the side, a look of complete indifference in his eyes. "I could have died, Thor," Abigail said. If a dog could roll his eyes, Thor certainly would have then.

Abigail stood and brushed dead leaves from her jeans. She then joined Grandma, who stared at the house with a critical eye.

"What do you think?" Abigail asked.

"I think I'm grateful to have a granddaughter who conquers her fears just to help out her little old granny."

Abigail snickered. "So you don't mind that the lights aren't exactly symmetrical?"

"I don't even mind that you mixed up the strands of clear bulbs with the multi-colored ones."

Abigail looked up and down the street. Even in the gray light of the late fall morning, she could see that all the other houses were festooned with lights, nativities, snowmen, Santa Clauses, and every other Christmas-themed decoration their neighbors could think of. Stiff competition.

"Now," Grandma said, her eyes bright and mischievous. "What are you going to wear for your date?"

"*My* date? If anything, you and Willy are the ones going on a date. I'm just chaperoning."

"Chaperoning with the help of a tall, dark, and handsome James."

Abigail playfully pinched Grandma's arm. "You just won't quit, will you?"

"I'm very persistent, as you know. Now, come inside and have a cup of hot cocoa and a cookie. Date or not, I'm sure we've got a fabulous evening ahead of us. Shingo Yamamoto is equal parts genius, artist, and toymaker."

CHAPTER TWO

Grandma and Abigail set out that evening bundled up like snowmen against the cold. The sun had set, so the two made their way by the light of the stars—not to mention the endless Christmas lights.

It seemed that every streetlight, every evergreen bush, and every leafless tree was draped with a kaleidoscope of lights. Abigail could understand the wild abandon the homeowners had used with their own lots; what she couldn't understand was the near chaos of décor on public sidewalks, parks, and benches.

"Grandma, is it just me, or does it look like a pack of Santa's elves drank too much eggnog and decided to decorate Wallace Point?"

Grandma walked daintily, her soft cheeks burrowed into the folds of her pink scarf. "Oh, don't be such a Scrooge."

"I'm not being a Scrooge! I'm just saying this town could maybe save a couple of decorations for the rest of the country."

"Ha! No chance. This is Wallace Point, where we do Christmas right."

"Jeez, if I didn't know any better, I would say you've been practicing that line."

"Of course I have. I say it every winter to every tourist who comes into the shop."

Downtown Wallace Point was just as bright and full of good cheer as the surrounding neighborhoods. Every store window boasted elaborate winter displays. Even Kirby Madsen, owner of the Madsen Candlepin Lanes, had deigned to hang an evergreen wreath on the front door.

But it was Mr. Yamamoto's Toys and Games that had lured customers out into the cold evening. As Grandma and Abigail approached the usually quiet store, they had a moment to appreciate the strong turnout.

"Wow," Abigail said. "I never expected so many people to show up to this thing. There are so many faces I don't know."

Grandma smiled knowingly. "I rather thought this might happen. I wasn't joking earlier when I said Shingo was part genius. I wouldn't be surprised if a few collectors from around the country aren't wandering around in the crowd."

"You mean Mr. Yamamoto is that well-known?"

"Oh my, yes! Shingo is the best at what he does. Look there." Grandma motioned with her head. "See the man with the potbelly?"

Abigail scanned the crowd. "I see a lot of potbellies."

"Not like this one you don't."

"Oh, is it the enormous potbelly under the black sweater covered with crumbs?"

"That's the one. I think I see a stripe of mustard there too."

"Yep, we're on the same page."

"Good. Anyhow, that gentleman is one of those collectors. Years ago, he tried to buy several pieces of mine that he was missing from his collection."

The owner of the potbelly was a middle-aged man with a shiny forehead and a half-eaten hot dog in one hand. He was sidling up to groups of people here and there, engaging them in conversation, but never for very long before moving on to the next group.

"He seems like he's on a mission," Abigail remarked.

"Well," said a familiar voice behind them. "If it isn't Wallace Point's loveliest antique dealers."

Abigail and Grandma whirled to find James, dressed in his usual trench coat, and his father, Sheriff Wilson.

"Willy!" Grandma threw her arms out to give the man a hug. She was one of the few people in town who called him by his nickname, and Abigail noticed the endearment always made the older man blush.

"How are you, Florence? And Abigail?" he asked.

"We're a bit on the cold side, but nothing to worry about," Grandma answered. "Anything interesting going on over at the station?"

"Now, Florence, you know I'm not supposed to talk about work."

"Whatever you say, Willy." Grandma grinned cheekily, and Abigail couldn't help but join her. Willy was sweet on Grandma, and he had often used tough cases as an excuse to ask her for advice. Lucky for him, both Grandma and Abigail had a knack for solving tough cases. In fact, they'd already cracked two. As much as Willy claimed he wanted to shield Grandma from any more crime, Abigail knew Grandma always got her way.

"Grandma was just telling me about how super-famous Mr. Yamamoto is."

"Those weren't my exact words," Grandma pointed out, "but Shingo is undoubtedly celebrated in certain circles. The word is that today's theme is Myth and Mystery."

James turned to Abigail. "Have you had a chance to look at his stuff?"

"Not as much as I'd like. I remember seeing a display not too long ago. I think it was during The Last Hurrah."

Wallace Point, small and quaint, survived on the tourist dollars that came in over summer and Christmas, but that didn't mean that the locals didn't miss their peace and quiet. The Last Hurrah was an annual tradition, a final fling before the town was given over to tourists.

"I loved his creations as a kid," James said, his gaze faraway and dreamy.

"I'd say you still do," Sheriff Wilson commented. "Dragging me all the way out here for some wooden toys."

Grandma narrowed her eyes. "Oh, stop it. You know these aren't just wooden toys." She turned to Abigail. "Mr. Yamamoto grew up here and he's one of the brightest children I've ever known. Since he was a youngster, maybe thirteen or fourteen, he's been making his automata—and they just keep getting finer and more complex. I really thought he would leave for bigger and better things, but after college, he came right back here and set up shop. Now he's married and has a bright young child of his own who's following pretty confidently in his footsteps."

"Look," James said, almost reverently. "Mr. Yamamoto's opening the door."

Abigail didn't bother to try to catch sight of the toy maker over the crowd. James was at least a foot taller than her; there was no way she could compete with his view.

Instead, she felt the crowd around her shift and compress as eager customers pushed their way forward. Elbows jostled her away from Grandma, and for a moment, Abigail was lost in the midst of the mass. That was when she noticed a woman in a red coat.

Somewhere in her thirties, the woman sulked at the outskirts of the crowd. Her candy-apple coat reached her shins, and it seemed to be clumsily concealing something beneath. The woman kept looking under her coat, then looking up and around her, as if she were worried about being seen. On one of her quick glances around, she locked eyes with Abigail. Feeling awkward, Abigail looked away for a brief moment. When she looked back, the woman in red had disappeared.

A hand reached out of the crowd and grabbed her own. "I've got you, Cupcake." James grinned down at her. "You and your Grandma are hard to keep track of in a group of normal-sized people. Come on."

Usually Abigail would put up a fuss, but James teasing her was nothing new. And at least if she stuck with him, she'd find Grandma again.

CHAPTER THREE

James guided Abigail through the crowd and into the store, when they both stopped dead in their tracks, shocked by what they saw.

Above their heads flapped an enormous bird. It sported golden feathers, its glassy eyes burning a fiery red. The bird made no sound except for its wings, which beat the air serenely, methodically.

"It's a phoenix," James murmured. Abigail heard him, even through the noise of the crowd, and she couldn't help but smile when she saw his face. He had that silly grin she was growing fond of and his eyes were far away again. Abigail figured he was somewhere in his boyhood, when his world had been whole and magic was still possible. James continued, "Do you know the myth of this one?"

"It's a bird that's reborn every five hundred years from the ashes of its predecessor."

James laughed. "You're like a walking, talking encyclopedia. I was just going to say it was a fire bird."

"As an antique dealer, I need to know these odd little details. Oh, look!" Abigail pointed up at the bird. Without any fanfare, real flames crawled up the dazzling wings. In just a few seconds, the flames chewed through the feathers, leaving only a torso. Golden ash floated down onto the customers, many of whom weren't even aware of the spectacle going on over their heads.

Without the distraction of the wings, Abigail could now see the wooden rod from which the bird had been suspended. It had been painted white to blend in with the ceiling, and even now it continued swinging slowly around and around.

Then, as quietly as the first phoenix had disappeared, a new one appeared. Fresh feathers, now gold tinged with orange, unfurled from the torso still attached to the wooden rod and flapped serenely again.

"How did he do that?" Abigail asked breathlessly.

"Maybe we'll never know. Myth and Mystery, remember?" James ginned and nudged her with his elbow. "How many people can say they've seen a phoenix rise from its ashes? I remember this store was always full of surprises like that. When I was really little, Mom would bring me here and I would search every corner for one of Mr. Yamamoto's hidden wonders. I was so afraid I'd miss out on one."

Abigail looked at the faces of the people around her. Some were familiar, many weren't. But everyone's eyes glowed, and the sound of laughter drowned out the Christmas music playing in the background.

"Well," Abigail declared. "This December already beats all the ones I had in Boston."

"Look. There's your Grandma."

"Where?"

"With Shingo," James reported from his tall vantage point. "He's handing her a bag, and now she's giving him money. Looks a bit like a drug deal if you ask me. If Dad weren't right next to her, I'd be a little worried."

"Maybe you still should be. I'm pretty sure Grandma has Sheriff Wilson wrapped around her little finger. Come on."

Abigail dragged James over through the crowd to the far end of the store. Grandma's face, already bright and happy, shone even brighter when she caught sight of Abigail and James.

"There you two are! Come here and meet Shingo."

Shingo Yamamoto was a lean man with dark, attentive eyes and a hint of a smile on his lips. Grandma touched his shoulder.

"Shingo, I'd like you to meet Abigail, my granddaughter. Abigail, this is Mr. Yamamoto."

Shingo took Abigail's hand firmly in his and said simply, "Please, call me Shingo. James, it's good to see you again after so many years."

James's eyes widened. "You remember me? I haven't been

here in maybe two decades."

"I always remember my best customers."

"I bet you say that to everyone," James laughed, but his eyes were hopeful. Shingo only smiled.

"It's nice to meet you, Shingo," Abigail jumped in. "The phoenix was incredible."

"Thank you. You saw it before it turned to ash?"

"Luckily, yes. Did you, Grandma?"

"No," Grandma said, and then she patted the bag Shingo had given her. "But I think I might have one. Shingo is kind enough to always put aside a full set of his creations for me. He discontinues his designs after just six months, so there's a rush to buy them."

"Do you have a complete collection?" James asked

Grandma sighed. "I wish I did. I missed out on a few sets and have been paying dearly ever since, as I've tried to track them down."

Just then, a slender girl with Shingo's intelligent eyes walked up to Grandma. "Hi, Granny Lane! Want to see what I'm working on?"

Grandma leaned down to the young girl's height. "A Hanako original? I wouldn't miss it! But first, let me introduce you to some special people." Grandma shifted so that Hanako was now in the center of the group. "James and Abigail, this is Hanako, Shingo's daughter. She's only eight and already has her own little workshop. Hanako, this is James Wilson, Sheriff Wilson's son. And this is Abigail Lane, my granddaughter."

Shock registered on the little girl's face. "You have a granddaughter?"

"How else would I be Granny Lane?"

Hanako, understanding quickly, broke into a sheepish smile. "Yeah, I guess that makes sense. My workshop is this way."

James gave Abigail a nudge. "I'm going to look around with my father. You guys have fun."

"You too."

With that, little Hanako marched through the crowd, leading Grandma and Abigail to the back of the store. They entered a narrow hallway that had just two doors: one on the left, which was secured with a heavy padlock, and one on the right, which had a handwritten sign stating, "Hanako's Workstation."

Hanako pushed open the door to the workshop, leaving Abigail to wonder about the locked door opposite it. Why would Shingo need a padlock? Was he working on something that was top secret?

The moment she walked into Hanako's room, however, Abigail forgot all about the door on the left.

Above their heads hovered a multitude of metal butterflies with iridescent wings. In the corners, birds hung serenely, waiting for their moment to fly like the phoenix. All over Hanako's worktable, wooden bumblebees of varying sizes loitered quietly.

Everything was still until Hanako moved through the workshop, touching a lever here, winding a crank there.

Slowly, the room fluttered to life. A dozen wings began to beat with the touch of Hanako's small hand.

Abigail finally found her voice and said, "This is incredible, Hanako. How do you do it?"

Hanako grinned. "Magic. Mystery. And maybe just a little bit of engineering. Take a look at my hummingbird!"

The girl made her way to her worktable and gently pushed a host of bumblebees away from a complex automaton. Hanako wound a little wheel, and the bird dipped its slender beak deep into a flower before easing away again, its wings undulating gracefully all the while.

Abigail could hardly believe her eyes even though all the turning wheels and moving parts were completely exposed. The movements were so fluid, so realistic, that Abigail couldn't understand how it had been made by a child.

"It's lovely," Grandma cooed, wrapping Hanako in a big hug. "I can see you're still into birds, bees, and butterflies."

The girl nodded emphatically. "The three Bs! Miss Bellerose says we wouldn't have flowers without them."

Suddenly, a loud explosion ripped through the air, followed by a guttural yell. Abigail immediately ducked, yanking Grandma and Hanako down with her and pulling them under the worktable. Huddled together, Abigail's eyes met Grandma's. She saw fear, surprise, and a frightening amount of anger.

That was definitely a gunshot. And if the scream was any indication, there was a victim nearby.

CHAPTER FOUR

H anako tried to scramble to her feet, crying, "Papa!"
Grandma clamped her hand down on Hanako's
thin arm. "Hanako, no! Stay here. Stay quiet. Understand?"

Hanako looked up into Grandma's usually gentle eyes
and saw steely determination. Choking back a little sob,
Hanako nodded, then buried her face in her hands.

As the immediate shock of the gunshot passed, a fire
flared in Abigail's belly. Who would shoot a gun, and at such
a special occasion?

Abigail peeked out from under the worktable. She could
hear screams coming from the front of the store, as well as
the urgent, authoritative voices of Sheriff Wilson and James.
But she had no idea what was happening in the hallway,
where the gunfire seemed to come from.

It had only been a few seconds since the crack of the gun,

and she was pretty sure she hadn't heard any footsteps running down the hall.

That was when she remembered the locked door.

Abigail broke away from Grandma and Hanako, peering out through the crack of the ajar workshop door. The hallway beyond seemed shadowy in comparison to the well-lit workroom, but Abigail could just make out the door opposite her. The padlock now hung open.

Footsteps pattered down the hallway as Sheriff Wilson appeared, his pistol drawn, James right at his heels. The sheriff caught sight of Abigail and called out in a low, steady voice, "You all right?"

Abigail nodded. "Yeah. It's me, Grandma, and Hanako in here. None of us are hurt."

"Where'd the gunshot come from?" James asked, his face serious and inscrutable. Abigail jerked her chin toward the door across the hall. The sheriff moved forward smoothly, setting his back against the wall next to the door.

"Hanako?" called a voice from down the hall.

"Papa!" Hanako tried to jump up, but Grandma held her fast again.

"Let me see Hanako!" Shingo snapped as he tried to push past James. "Is she all right?"

"She's okay," James said, holding Shingo back. "Listen, is there any other way into that room?"

"Let me go to my daughter."

Sheriff Wilson commanded, "Mr. Yamamoto, please understand that this is possibly an active crime scene. Until we figure out who discharged a weapon in your store, none of us are safe. Cooperate with us, and let's make sure Hanako is actually out of harm's way."

A tense moment passed until Shingo finally said, "There's no other way into that room. Not even a window."

Willy nodded. "Florence," he called into the workroom. "Keep everyone in there. James, keep Shingo at a safe distance." In one fluid motion, he lowered his gun, kicked the door open, then swung the pistol back up. After a moment he stepped into the room.

"Clear," he called over his shoulder. "But there's a body."

"A body?" Shingo's voice was hoarse with shock.

Abigail heard a scuffle in the hallway. Acting on an impulse, she met Grandma's gaze. Grandma nodded, and Abigail poked her head further out the door.

"I'm sorry, Mr. Yamamoto," James was saying as he blocked Shingo's progress down the hallway. "I'm really sorry, but this is a crime scene now. You'll have to stay back."

With James distracted by Shingo, Abigail saw her chance to get a closer look. She crossed the hallway and peered into the room, seeing a man's limp body stretched out on the floor. The man's hands were clasped over his abdomen, where the bullet must've hit him.

Abigail's head swam. She'd never seen a murdered body before, and she wasn't exactly happy to see one now. Still, she steadied herself and tried to pick up as many details as she could.

The pungent odor of smoke caught in her nose. She

noticed a toy cannon sitting on the floor against the wall directly in front of the body. Next to the cannon was a little pile of smoking springs, screws, and what looked like gunpowder.

Abigail never imagined a toy cannon could kill a person, but then again, its barrel was a size comparable to a pistol. The question now was: who had fired it?

Another quick glance around the room told her that aside from Sheriff Wilson and the body, the room was empty. Shingo hadn't lied; the once-padlocked door was the only way in and out.

Sheriff Wilson had been standing inside the room, absorbing the scene just as Abigail had. After a moment, he closed the distance between himself and the body, then crouched down.

He pressed his fingers on the man's neck to check for a pulse, only to yank his hand back as the man violently sprung to life, coughing and wheezing. The man took in a final breath to say, "Shingo... Shingo did this to me."

He then went limp, and his chest settled for the last time.

CHAPTER FIVE

Sheriff Wilson stood up slowly, looking rather dazed until he caught sight of Abigail peering at him from the door. "Abigail Lane," he groaned. "I told you to stay in that room."

Abigail backed away, knowing she was pushing her luck. He stepped out into the hallway after her, before noticing Shingo making another attempt to get past James.

"Let me see my daughter," Shingo demanded, his voice like shattered glass.

James maintained his poise. "I'm sorry, Mr. Yamamoto, but this is a crime scene." Finally, Shingo relented, his arms crossed in worry.

"All right then," began Sheriff Wilson. "Get a hold of the station, James."

James whipped out his phone and immediately started

dialing. As he spoke with the station, Hanako moved from Grandma's protective arms and poked her head out the door, seeing her father. "Can I stand with my dad, Mr. Wilson?"

Sheriff Wilson's shoulders slumped. It was as if he had been shocked enough to kick into high gear for a few seconds. But at the sound of the little girl's voice, that energy had been sapped away. All that was left was sadness and frustration.

"Hanako, you can stand by your father," he said at last. "For now. Be careful not to touch anything. Shingo, where's Madeline?"

"She left ten minutes ago to grab some takeout." Shingo glumly looked down at Hanako, ruffling her hair. "The grand reopening had really worked up an appetite for us."

Abigail glanced at Grandma and whispered, "Madeline?"

"His wife," Grandma whispered back.

Shingo picked up Hanako and rested her on his hip as if she were still a toddler. The girl's scrawny legs, wrapped in fuzzy, hot pink leggings, reached down almost to his knees. He smoothed her hair away from her face and kissed her tear-soaked eyelashes. "It'll be okay, Hanako," he whispered to her.

James tucked his phone back into his pocket and told his father, "Police are on their way. I'll go make sure the store is cleared out and that everyone stays nearby for questioning."

"Yes," Sheriff Wilson said with a nod. "I'll watch these four." James took off, and the sheriff turned to Shingo. "I'm going to try to be delicate since your daughter is here. But where were you when the gunfire went off?"

"I… I had stepped outside for a moment to see Madeline off."

"Who can confirm that besides your wife?"

"I don't know. Maybe a customer saw me head out."

Sheriff Wilson regarded him for a moment before shaking his head. "Abigail, I know you were poking your head into the room when I checked the victim's pulse. Did you hear what he said?"

Abigail clenched her jaw. She looked at Hanako's wide-eyed expression and wished she hadn't been a witness. Then, reluctantly, she met Shingo's gaze. His eyes were troubled, but his look was gentle. Abigail took a deep breath and said, "I heard an unproven accusation."

"Thank you, Abigail. Shingo Yamamoto, I'm afraid that once your wife returns and takes Hanako, you must take a walk with me."

"Sheriff Wilson—" Abigail began.

"Willy!" Grandma just about growled.

Sheriff Wilson gave them both a sharp look and they both fell silent.

Grandma stood beside Abigail now, looking like she might burst into a thousand angry pieces. James returned just before she could say something, with a small woman following behind him.

James announced, "Madeline was just returning when I got everybody outside."

The small woman behind James wore a tightly controlled expression, her face almost like a mask as she tried to peer over his shoulder. When she saw Hanako and Shingo, her façade slipped. Her eyes filled with tears, and her chin trembled.

The reunited family clung to each other while Abigail and the others watched.

Sheriff Wilson cleared his throat. "Shingo, I'm sorry, but we've got to take that walk now. James, bring the ladies out. We need to start processing the scene."

"Yes, sir."

Shingo passed a reluctant Hanako over to Madeline, who looked at Shingo with questioning eyes. He whispered something in her ear that made her laugh and then burst into more tears. Then he followed Sheriff Wilson down the hall.

The woman turned to James as he herded the four of them out. "What's going on? Why did Sheriff Wilson take... He doesn't think Shingo... What's in that room?"

"Something terrible has happened in that room," Grandma said. "But I don't believe for a second that Shingo had anything to do with it."

"Neither do I," Abigail added quietly.

James gave them both a look before saying, "Madeline, we don't know what happened yet. We're still trying to process all the details."

Tears rolled down Madeline's cheeks, though her expression was one of determination. She looked at Grandma, at James, then at Abigail in turn. "I know Shingo would never hurt anyone or anything. He creates. He doesn't destroy."

"Come on," James coaxed her. "We're almost outside."

As they exited, they were greeted by a young sharp-eyed police officer who had just arrived onto the scene. "James," he said in recognition.

"Officer Reynolds," James replied back as he looked over the scene. Police were already swarming the place. Several patrol cars were parked in front of the store, their lights flashing. Other officers were rounding up the crowd, taking names, and setting up tape around the store.

Officer Reynolds waved them away from the crime scene and out onto the cold, dark street. "Sheriff Wilson told me to keep an eye on you four. He'll be back soon, once he's done questioning the perp."

Perp? Abigail shot James a look and whispered just loud enough for only him to hear, "Shingo's already being called a 'perp'?"

He responded just as quietly, so Madeline and Hanako couldn't hear, "I suppose so. I mean, having the murder victim accuse you right before he died kinda makes you the number one suspect."

Abigail groaned. "I could point you to a couple of suspicious-looking characters if you really need a suspect."

"Don't get too riled up yet. If he didn't do it, he has nothing to worry about, okay? Let the process do its thing."

"Yeah, because the process has never put an innocent man behind bars before."

James opened his mouth, then quickly thought better of it. "Anyway, I'm going to double-check the store's perimeter for any other points of entry."

"I hope you find something." Abigail turned back to Grandma, Hanako, and Madeline as James stalked off. The four of them had nothing to say as they watched the police take control of the scene.

A minute later, another officer whisked off Madeline and Hanako, leaving Grandma and Abigail where they were. Abigail took this opportunity to scan the crowd. The gathering of people hadn't thinned since being forced out. If anything, it was getting bigger.

She looked around for suspicious faces. If Shingo wasn't the killer, that meant someone else was, and that someone else could still be lingering nearby.

The familiar faces, those of the residents of Wallace Point, registered shock and sadness. It seemed that Shingo Yamamoto was well-loved by his neighbors. The unfamiliar faces in the crowd showed a greedy sort of curiosity. Abigail shivered, then caught sight of a familiar potbelly.

The potbellied collector from earlier was no longer accosting person after person. Instead, he watched the police intently. Abigail followed his gaze, seeing that he was staring at the young officer from earlier, Officer Reynolds. The collector visibly stirred when Sheriff Wilson reappeared and gave Officer Reynolds two bulky evidence bags.

A memory suddenly tugged at Abigail's mind. She looked around again, but couldn't find what she was looking for.

The woman with the candy apple coat—where had she gone? And what had she been hiding under her coat just before the store opened?

Grandma sighed. Abigail nudged her encouragingly. "Don't worry, Grandma," she whispered. "It's not over until you and I say it's over."

Grandma frowned slightly as she considered it, then she nodded. "That's right, isn't it? I nearly forgot." After watching the crowd for a few more minutes, Grandma nodded toward the street. "Let's go back home. We've got a busy week or two ahead of us, so we'll need our rest."

Abigail smiled. "That's more like it."

CHAPTER SIX

U sually when Abigail went on her morning run with Thor and Missy, she set a slow, steady pace. The morning after Shingo's arrest, however, she channeled all her frustration into her legs.

Her feet pounded the pavement, her throat and lungs ached from the cold air, and her energy carried her farther than she thought it could.

Her legs gave out right as she approached Camille Bellerose's house. Camille was a wisp of a woman who taught at the local elementary school and prided herself on growing enormous vegetables, usually gourds.

Even now, despite the frosted grass and cloudy sky, Camille was out in her front garden, crawling on her hands and knees around the resting garden beds.

SHELLY WEST

"What's there left to do," Abigail called from the sidewalk, "now that it's winter?"

Camille got up from her knees and smacked her hands together to shake off any lingering dirt. "You've got to keep the plants company, if nothing else."

Abigail smiled as she remembered the first time she'd seen Camille. The woman had been whispering sweet nothings to a host of foliage. "Right. I always forget how much plants like conversation. Maybe instead of giving the houseplants too much water, I should try talking to them."

"That would definitely be a start." Camille took a moment to study Abigail's face, then looked down at Missy and Thor, who had both collapsed onto a nice cool patch of grass. "You've been running pretty hard. Trying to keep up with James?"

"No way."

"Yeah, he's surprisingly quick for someone so tall. He runs maybe half an hour earlier than you do. Why don't you two ever go running together?"

Abigail laughed and rolled her eyes. "If you knew how Grandma would react to me and him spending any extra time together..."

"I thought she liked James."

"She does! That's the thing. She's always trying to get us together. But I just want things to settle down a bit more for me, you know?"

"Yeah, it was a pretty big move you made, coming from Boston."

"Right? Not to mention—" Abigail cut herself off.

"What is it?"

"It's stupid. But naturally there's a bit of tension, considering my tendency to... well, get a little too involved in things."

"Like the last two murders?"

"Yeah. And James, of course, is always looking out for his father. Even if that means arresting an innocent man."

Camille drew closer to Abigail and lowered her voice, as if there might be eavesdroppers. "Yeah, I heard you were there last night. So you don't think Shingo did it?"

"I don't. Not that I can prove it, but I really can't see him doing it. I've dealt with liars, people trying to get away with fraud, and I can just tell he isn't the type."

Camille nodded. "I don't think he did it either. You know, I was going to drop by there a little later yesterday, but by the time I got there, the police were out in full force. I was supposed to see Hanako's latest hummingbird."

Tears sprang to Abigail's eyes, catching her off guard. She'd never been the emotional type, except for maybe her temper. But something about Hanako having her father taken from her really got to Abigail. "I got to see her hummingbirds and all her other creations just before everything happened. They were amazing. At her age, I could maybe manage to glue a couple of popsicle sticks together."

"Hanako's a special one, all right. She's one of my best students."

"If there's anything I can do to help her, let me know."

Abigail paused, before finishing lamely, "I don't know what helping her would look like, but just let me know."

"I will. And you let me know too. Anything you can think of to make her Christmas a little brighter."

They said their goodbyes, and Abigail started off again with Thor and Missy, who were getting antsy in the cold. Back at the store, Abigail was greeted with the smell of freshly roasted coffee.

She ran upstairs and showered, then hurried back down to the kitchen. Grandma was making breakfast so Abigail portioned out Thor and Missy's food before setting the table. Soon, the plates were laden with hot oatmeal, fresh fruit, and vegetable omelets.

"Nice spread, Grandma. You expecting company?"

"Not at all. I'm just in a terrible mood. Sometimes eating helps."

Abigail plopped down into a chair at the small kitchen table. "I know what you mean. I'm still frustrated over last night. The victim blaming Shingo, not saying anything else besides, 'He did it.' Not very helpful. And then I'm mad at myself for essentially becoming a witness. I mean, who knows how far this will go? What if I have to testify against Shingo about what I heard?"

"Oh, goodness, let's hope it doesn't come to that." Grandma dished fruit into her oatmeal and added a dollop of jam as a sweetener. She mixed it all together, then shoveled several bites into her mouth. Her eyes rested on the jam jar, even though her gaze seemed unfocused. "I wish Willy would have given Shingo's family at least some reassurance before taking him in. It's just so cold, arresting him without a word in front of his family, then hauling him off while they have to pick up the pieces."

"I know James and Sheriff Wilson were just doing their jobs. I know the last thing the sheriff wants is to muddy up the crime scene, or lead any potential witnesses. But still, it would have been nice if he had said something, or had even given us a look like, 'Yeah, I know this is screwed up.'"

Grandma shook her head in disappointment. "What if he isn't questioning Shingo's guilt?"

"Then you and I will have to give him a stern talking-to."

They finished the rest of their breakfast in silence, then proceeded to open the store. It was a busy day at Whodunit Antiques. Some of the collectors who'd come to Wallace Point just for Shingo's re-opening apparently decided to stick around a few days. That, combined with the ever-increasing number of Christmastime tourists as well as locals who wanted to swap murder details, meant Grandma and Abigail had their hands full.

Abigail was grateful for the work, however. Engaging customers and attempting to do mental math helped her gain a bit of distance from her feelings. That, and she took every opportunity to let strangers and neighbors alike know she believed in Shingo's innocence.

So, when James knocked on their front door a little while after closing, Abigail had managed to calm down just enough to let him in from the cold.

"Hey, Cupcake," he said, taking off his coat and hanging it on the nearby rack.

"James. Grandma and I are set up in the living room. Want something to drink?"

"Anything hot would be great." He spoke easily, but Abigail could sense an underlying tension in his voice.

Grandma walked in, saying, "You two go on into the living room while I make hot cocoa."

"No, Grandma, it's all right. I can make it." Abigail was calm enough to let James in, but she wasn't sure she wanted to face him yet.

"Nonsense. I need to stretch these old bones of mine anyway."

"I really don't mind. In fact, I think I need the practice."

"Well, that's certainly true, but don't practice on us tonight. Now, go on."

"Ladies, ladies," James cut in, his smile a little sad. "Now, don't go tripping over yourselves to keep me company, okay?"

Abigail sighed and led him into the living room. Missy jumped onto Grandma's chair by the fire, so Abigail took the chair opposite Grandma's, while James sank into the low couch. An awkward silence followed until James leaned forward.

"Abigail, let's talk about last night."

"Maybe we should give it some time. I'm not exactly the cool-headed type."

James laughed. "Trust me, I know. You and Granny Lane have a lot in common."

"Thanks. That's a compliment to me."

"As it was intended to be. Look, I'm going to get right to the point. I know you wanted me and my father to let Shingo walk last night, but a murder scene like that, with an immediate accusation from the murder victim himself... well, my father had to take precautions."

"I know. I just wish it didn't happen that way." Abigail felt the fire in her belly again. "His family was right there. Hanako probably picked up on the fact that a man was murdered in the room next to her workshop. Her mother too, having to hold it all together by herself..."

James shook his head, his eyes on the roaring fire before them. "I'm not going to argue with that. It's getting close to Christmas. His grand reopening was ruined. Maybe we even hurt his reputation by taking him away in front of everyone." He turned his gaze back to Abigail. "But he had the key to the padlock when we checked his pockets. He was missing for a few minutes before the gunshot, according to witnesses. Then we have the murder victim's accusation. We can't just let him walk. Not yet. But we're doing our best to find any reason to let him go. Trust me. Dad isn't happy about what he had to do."

"I get that."

James added, "This kind of situation is one of the reasons I decided not to follow exactly in Dad's footsteps. Sometimes being a cop means you get to help people, but sometimes it means your hands are tied behind your back. The law can be a little cold sometimes."

Abigail stared at the fire for a long moment. "Thanks for giving me space last night. I probably would have chewed your head off."

"Yeah, I could see that coming from a mile away. You Lanes are pretty predictable. Why do you think Dad isn't here with me?"

"Because he knows what's good for him," Grandma said, breezing in with a tray of steaming mugs. "Okay, tell us everything you learned today."

James gladly accepted his hot cocoa and took a sip before proceeding. "Dad gave me strict orders not to involve you two in yet another murder case... *But* you're 2-0 right now, so I don't see why not. Just don't tell him I said anything."

"Deal," Abigail said.

"Well, here's the kicker," James began. "Here's the main reason we can't let Shingo go yet. I was saving it for when Granny Lane came in."

"Okay," Grandma prodded. "What is it?"

"Shingo isn't acting exactly innocent. He won't answer any of our questions, and he keeps mumbling the weirdest things."

Grandma exchanged a frown with Abigail before asking, "Like what?"

"At one point he said something about a murderous automaton. Then, when Dad said the toy cannon didn't exactly qualify as an automaton, Shingo said something about self-immolation and then just stopped talking. We didn't get anything else out of him."

"What in the world could any of that mean?" Grandma asked, and they sat in silence as they pondered it.

"A murderous automaton," Abigail mused aloud after a few moments. "A wooden automaton that pulled the cannon's trigger... then set itself on fire to eliminate the evidence?"

"That would be rather unusual," Grandma said. "But it would be within Shingo's abilities to make."

"I remember there being a pile of ash by the toy cannon. I thought it was just gunpowder, but that doesn't make any sense now that I think about it. Could it have been the ashes of an automaton after it ignited itself? Can an automaton even fire a cannon?"

James shrugged. "It's very possible. In the toy cannon's case, you wouldn't even need to squeeze a trigger. It's a string you pull, which is a basic enough movement to automate. And the automaton did leave something behind besides ash: some screws and springs. Automata need, at the very least, a spring to store and expel energy for movement."

"I hate to admit it," Abigail said, "but a self-immolating automaton doesn't look great for Shingo. He's the only person in town who could build something like that."

Grandma sipped her cocoa, seeming less convinced than Abigail. "Do we know who the victim is?"

James shook his head. "We couldn't find any identification on him, and so far, nobody has been able to put a name to his face."

"An out-of-towner, then," Grandma concluded. Every local face in Wallace Point was known—that much was for sure.

"The mystery only gets worse from there. Remember how Dad kicked down the door?"

Abigail recalled it. "Yeah. Didn't he do that to get the jump on whoever was inside?"

"No. He tried the doorknob before that, but it was locked from the inside. He told me this after. So, it's a room with only one way in, and it was locked, presumably by the murder victim. Odd, isn't it?"

That got Abigail thinking. "What if this is all just an accident? What if the automaton was just supposed to warn away who tried to enter the room? Like some sort of quirky security measure? Maybe the murder victim locked the door behind him, planning to steal some stuff, then set off the automaton security system."

James shrugged. "I guess that's possible, but why wouldn't Shingo just explain that to us? Besides, a cannon aimed right at the door is more of a trap than a security measure. Which reminds me, the cannon's missing too. Dad told me that I was *especially* not allowed to tell you that, but…"

Abigail's mouth dropped open. "What?"

"Yeah. The screws, springs, and ash from the automaton are still in police possession since they were put in a different evidence bag, but the toy cannon is apparently gone."

"Does evidence go missing a lot in this town or what?" Abigail asked in disbelief. "Remember that collector we dealt with? He had somehow gotten the Ripper's knife from police evidence too."

"It is a bit odd," James conceded.

"Who do you think could have stolen it?"

"Well, I said it was missing, not stolen."

Abigail arched an eyebrow. "That kind of evidence doesn't just go missing."

Grandma chimed in, "There are at least a dozen avid automata collectors in Wallace Point right now who would gladly break the law to get that cannon. I can think of one in particular who has already been a nuisance."

Abigail nodded. "Oh, that's right! Mr. Potbelly!"

James blinked. "Mr. Potbelly?"

"You'd understand if you saw him," Grandma explained. "I don't remember his actual name, unfortunately, but I have seen Mr. Potbelly here before. The man doesn't know when to quit. I used to display one of Shingo's earlier creations with a sign clearly stating it wasn't for sale, and I swear he was making plans to break into the store to get it. I ended up having to move the little guy up to my attic for its own safety."

James shrugged. "Guess I'll inform Dad about him and go see if Mr. Potbelly has popped up in places he shouldn't have."

Abigail figured she had nothing to lose in asking, "You don't have any pictures of the crime scene you could share with me, do you? Specifically photos of the cannon and left-over springs?"

"Let's not forget the screws too," James noted. "But I don't know if I should be sharing photos."

"Grandma's pretty familiar with Shingo's creations. Maybe a detail in the photos could give us an interesting lead."

James took in a deep breath, his internal struggle evident on his face. "Fine. Just keep it between the three of us, okay?" He whipped out his phone and texted her a picture before standing. "Okay. If you come up with anything, shoot me a text. And now, ladies, my sweet motel room awaits me. Thank you for the cocoa, Granny Lane."

"Thank you for the information, James. It's nice having you over again."

"If only because I give you more details than my father does," James said with a wink.

"For more reasons than that, dear." Grandma stood to pinch his cheek.

After he left, Abigail and Grandma sat and stared at the fire again. Thor took the spot James had vacated on the couch, and Missy snored loudly in Grandma's lap.

"What's on your mind, Abigail?"

Abigail hesitated. "It's a long shot, but I think I gotta go meet with someone. A source."

"A source I haven't thought of yet?"

"It's no one you know."

Grandma's mouth gaped as she demanded, "Someone *I* don't know? In Wallace Point? Who?"

"Just this weirdo. Don't worry, I'll take Thor with me for protection."

Grandma searched Abigail's face, then sighed. "Well, all right then. I'm sure you're sparing me the details so I don't worry. I won't pry. Just be careful."

"Of course, Grandma. You know me." Abigail then pulled out her phone, hoping she wouldn't regret what she was about to do next.

CHAPTER SEVEN

That following afternoon, Abigail sat hunched over at a picnic table at the local dog park. Thor had a handful of new friends to play with and he was enjoying himself immensely as he galloped around, leaving Abigail to shiver alone. She crossed her arms and bounced up and down, wishing she'd chosen a warmer location to rendezvous.

The man she emailed the night before had reluctantly helped her with her last case. He was a collector of "murderabilia," items connected to serial killers and their victims. While she normally wouldn't associate with people like that, this particular collector was a scrawny kid, hardly even Abigail's height. He had acted tough last time, but James easily broke him down. Abigail figured she could do the same, if need be.

In her email, however, she didn't let him know that they were acquaintances. She came up with a new screen name to proposition him from, going with the name "SilentNight" after having the Christmas song stuck in her head for a couple of hours. It sounded edgy enough for her intended audience too. From there, she had attached a cropped photo of the evidence and composed a straightforward message:

I hear you're a local collector of a particular kind of item. I'm in possession of the remaining pieces of the KILLER AUTOMATON associated in the most recent murder at Wallace Point. Picture attached. Interested?

    -SilentNight

In the morning, she'd woken up to a terse response:

I'm interested. $500, no questions asked. Blue Pier Gasoline Station. 3 p.m. tomorrow.

    -Lone Ronin

That moniker made Abigail snicker. Lone Ronin? The guy apparently hadn't realized how redundant that was. She emailed him back immediately that morning:

Too far. Meet me at the dog park in Wallace Point at 3 p.m. or I'll find another buyer. Cash only. How far away are you from Wallace Point?
    -SilentNight

A quick, lunchtime peek at her email revealed another message:

Thirty minutes. But I prefer meeting somewhere farther away from where I live.
    -Lone Ronin

To which Abigail had succinctly replied:

It's the park or nothing. Sit at the bench that faces north. Don't be late.
    -SilentNight

Now she waited. Abigail checked the time. 2:45 p.m. She stood, pulling Thor's leash out of her coat pocket. "Thor, come here, boy!"

At the sound of her voice, the tan Great Dane's ears perked up. He gave his playfellow a final, slobbery lick before turning and darting toward Abigail. She leashed him and together they started walking a brisk lap around the track that circled the dog park.

She pulled her hoodie over her head, attempting to bury her face in its depths. Then, she glanced at the other dog owners. With other people present, she doubted her guest would try anything funny.

At 3:00 p.m. sharp, she saw Lone Ronin's lanky figure lope into view. After looking about the park in the shiftiest way possible, he sat on the bench facing north, his face pallid in the bright afternoon. He didn't pay any particular attention to Abigail and Thor until she left the track, sat down beside him, pulled back her hoodie, and grinned.

It took him a moment to place her face. When he finally did, his eyes grew wide.

"Not you!" he moaned, jumping to his feet. "Not again!"

Lone Ronin took off toward the parking lot as fast as his skinny legs would take him.

Abigail nimbly unhooked Thor's leash from his collar, bent to his ear, and whispered fiercely, "Get him, Thor."

Thor exploded into a gallop. In no time flat, he'd caught up with the collector, seized him by his pant leg, and helped him to the ground. All in good fun, of course—at least for Thor. He always enjoyed a playful chase.

Lone Ronin, on the other hand, did not seem to enjoy rolling around in the grass with Thor. "Get this beast off me!" he whimpered as Thor licked his face.

Abigail leaned over him, making no moves to stop Thor.

"So we meet again, *Lone Ronin*. Last time you didn't give me a name."

"Get this crazy mutt off me, *please!*" the guy pleaded, his voice hardly more than a squeak.

Abigail feigned a gasp. "This isn't a mutt. Thor is a Great Dane, through and through. And he's quite the guard dog too."

"Please don't tell me you made me drive half an hour out here only to attack me with your dog and, once again, not deliver the goods you promised."

"You got that right, *Lone Ronin*."

"Stop calling me that," he moaned. "It's embarrassing."

"You called yourself that."

"Just call me Robbie. Jeez."

Abigail narrowed her eyes. "Robbie, huh? I don't know why, but I expected something more edgy."

"Look," Robbie began. He tried to shift his leg away from Thor, but the dog redoubled his grip on the pants and growled. Abigail could tell it was one of his playful growls, but she didn't share that with Robbie. "Honestly, lady, if you wanna talk murder weapons with me, just say so! You don't have to keep siccing your boyfriend and your dog on me."

Abigail chose not to correct him on the boyfriend bit, if only because it made her that much scarier to this kid. "Just say so, huh? Why would you willingly talk to me?"

"Because you've been up close and personal with two killers now!"

"How do you know that?"

"I looked you up after you ambushed me the first time. I don't know what it is about you, but you have a habit of mingling with murderers. I'll share what I know if you share some information yourself. All you have to do is ask from now on, okay?"

Abigail sighed. Having this guy help her willingly sure beat trying to squeeze information out of him. More importantly, some of the other dog owners were beginning to stare. She turned to Thor. "Let him go, boy. Seems like he's going to cooperate."

Thor released Robbie and licked his lips. Abigail pulled several treats from her pocket, which Thor scarfed down in no time.

"Okay," Robbie said as he stood and brushed off his pants. "What information were you about to try to interrogate out of me?"

"I want to know what you know about this most recent murder."

"Can do. But you need to give me some information I can work with in exchange."

"No," Abigail said simply.

Robbie shook his head. "You're not really great at bargaining, are you?"

"I bargain at my job. Off the clock, I demand."

"Fine, fine. I don't know anything about the automaton case yet, but I can give you a lead about that missing toy cannon. However, before I tell you that, I want something I can sink my teeth into. Come on, with both of the murder cases you helped solve, just give me one detail that can't be found in a newspaper."

Abigail figured she ought to throw him a bone, especially if he knew where the toy cannon might be. "Okay, what do you want to know?"

"Preferably something about the Ripper case." Robbie's pale face had a greedy expression, the same look she'd caught on the tourists who watched Shingo's arrest. The last thing Abigail wanted was to feed Robbie's appetite for the grotesque, especially at the expense of any victims. But she knew at least one interesting detail she was willing to share.

"The Ripper used to have an unofficial fan club here in Wallace Point. They followed his actions quite closely while he was still active. Even used to hang out at the cabin where he killed one of his victims. My mom was part of this fan club... Not that I'm proud of that."

"No way."

"And the reporter who initially broke the motel murder story? Well, she used to be in that club too. Now, about the missing murder weapon..."

"Fine, fine." Robbie looked around him suspiciously before leaning closer to Abigail. "We murderabilia collectors know about a guy on the Wallace Point police force who has a way of 'losing' evidence, so to speak."

"This guy's actually on the force? Right now?"

"Yeah. He's great."

"What's his name?"

"I can't tell you that! He'd kill me."

Abigail had half a mind to strong arm the poor kid again but it probably would have been better in the long run to earn his trust instead. So, she said, "Think you could maybe arrange a meeting with this police officer? Just the three of us?"

Robbie shifted uncomfortably. "I don't know about that. What do you plan to do to him?"

"Just talk. Honest." Abigail tried to put on a convincing smile.

"I don't know. I've been building up trust with him for a while, and knowing you, you'll shove him up against a wall or something."

"That was James. I wouldn't hurt a fly." When Robbie grimaced in response, Abigail considered a different approach. She knew the criminality of the act of buying evidence probably didn't faze Robbie, but somebody who liked to call himself Lone Ronin might have a different motivation she could prod at. "And besides, buying evidence from active investigations isn't very noble, is it? I thought a true murderabilia collector would have a bit more honor."

Robbie tilted his head. "Well, I mean... I guess. It's just more recent items are more valuable—"

"Interfering with active investigations, though? Don't you want the police to pin down the real killer? No point in collecting murderabilia if the police don't have the right guy, right?"

54

Robbie sighed dramatically. "You're really persistent. But you have a point, so fine, I'll talk to him." He then pointed at her, adding, "But I'm not promising anything."

Abigail smiled. "I'll keep in touch, Robbie."

CHAPTER EIGHT

The lead Robbie had given Abigail was a big one, but she couldn't exactly act on it. As much as she wanted to, she couldn't very well march down to the station and ask to see the officer guilty of selling evidence.

She was also reluctant to involve the Wilson men. Whoever the officer was, Sheriff Wilson was his superior, and James might be the guy's friend; James had seemed pretty chummy with the officers at the crime scene.

So, as impatient as Abigail was to clear Shingo's name and reunite him with his family, she had no choice but to wait on Robbie to set up a meeting—if the officer even agreed to it. That put Abigail back at square one, waiting for an idea, an opportunity, or for Shingo to actually tell the police he was innocent. Why he had yet to claim his innocence, Abigail couldn't begin to understand.

Luckily, Abigail had work to keep her busy. With Christmas fast approaching, the winter tourist season was in full swing. New faces, cheeks chafed by the cold, and eyes bright with holiday cheer streamed persistently into Whodunit Antiques. Every time Abigail finished helping one customer, she'd turn around to find three more waiting for her.

Finally, lunchtime came, and there were no customers waiting at the door. Abigail figured Grandma would take this opportunity to catch her breath, but instead, she started wandering about the store.

Abigail didn't think anything of it at first, until she heard Grandma muttering about lonely antiques as she disappeared behind a cluster of collectibles.

Frowning, Abigail followed her. "What are you talking about over there?"

Grandma jerked up. "Oh, I'm sorry, Abigail. I was in my own little world for a moment there. It's just that tonight is The Hanging, so I need to pick some freebies to leave out."

Abigail blinked. "Hanging? Freebies? What?"

"Oh," Grandma gasped. "You wouldn't know, would you? It's a Wallace Point tradition. The tourists just love it."

For a split second, Abigail had the odd and terrifying feeling she'd stepped between the pages of a Shirley Jackson story. Next, someone would ask how to spell her name for the town lottery. "Is somebody going to be *hanged*?"

"Goodness no! We're only hanging a cow, dear."

Abigail's voice squeaked. "What?"

"A papier-mâché cow! Oh dear. I really should start at the beginning, shouldn't I?"

"Uh, *yeah*."

Grandma chuckled. "Don't worry, no animals are harmed during the annual Wallace Point Hanging. It's a bit quirky, I suppose, but what isn't quirky about this town?"

"Good point."

"It started ages ago. A group of Lebeau pirates had their eyes on the supposed riches of the Wallace Point residents. But they didn't have the manpower or firepower to directly attack the city. So, they came up with an odd little scheme: they procured a cow and managed to hoist it up to hang from the church steeple."

Abigail's eyes widened. "That's not what I was expecting you to say. Why would they do that to some poor cow?"

"Well, the townspeople weren't expecting it either. Once word spread of the hoisted cow, everyone flocked to see it. With the stores and homes abandoned, the pirates waltzed right in and robbed everybody blind."

"Wow. Did the cow make it back to the ground unscathed?"

"That took some doing. But yes, the poor cow was eventually brought back down without any injury."

"Crazy."

"Right? That kind of history is too rich to let fade into the past. So every year during the winter tourist season, we reenact The Hanging. We don't use a real cow, of course. Like I said, we use a papier-mâché cow, which, over the years, has acquired a set of reindeer antlers, a harness of tinkling bells, and a red Rudolph nose."

"Only in Wallace Point."

Grandma laughed. "That's not all, though. When it's time to hoist the cow, all of us shopkeepers gather at the hanging, leaving free items outside for the tourists to 'steal.'"

"Is that what you were thinking about when you mentioned lonely antiques?"

"I didn't realize I said that out loud." The older woman blushed prettily. "But yes, that's what I meant. You see, the free items are usually cheap things like bookmarks or post-cards. After all, we can't expect Sally to gift one of her rare books, or for Kirby to give away bowling balls."

"Makes sense."

"I like to pick out old antiques that have been in the store for a while. It makes me sad to see some of them sit here without a home, collecting dust, so I pick a few dozen of them to leave out as a free offering."

Abigail shook her head. "Offerings, sacrificial papier-mâché cows, gatherings in the night... This whole thing sounds like a demonic ritual."

"Well, tourists can be quite the little demons sometimes, can't they? But they love the freebies, and these lonely antiques will finally find a good home."

"When is The Hanging?"

"Tonight! Would you like to join me for the hoist?"

"Um…" Abigail hedged. She honestly did think the whole tradition sounded pretty weird. But it would feel weirder to send Grandma out into the cold alone while she stayed in the house, listening to tourists fumble around on the front porch for freebies. Besides, the change in pace might help her come up with fresh ideas regarding the automaton murder. "Okay," she said at last. "I'll go. But don't be surprised if I seem pretty uncomfortable the whole time."

THE EVENING WAS SO cold that Abigail half-hoped Grandma would reconsider going to The Hanging. But the woman was bound and determined to go. She even wore a smile on her face, as if she enjoyed the prospect of going out into the frigid night. Abigail had no choice but to pull on an extra layer of everything and follow Grandma out the door.

The church used for the hanging was a quaint, white-clapboard chapel near downtown. For the occasion, the chapel had been decorated with what looked like millions of twinkling lights. The whole building blinked and glittered, and the light it provided was so bright, the group that gathered around it didn't need any other source of illumination.

Sally Kent, owner of the Book Cafe and good friend of Abigail's, had set up a coffee booth, and the local bakery had stocked her up with croissants, donuts, and brownies.

Grandma, never one to say no to sugar, made a beeline for Sally.

"Granny Lane!" Sally called, her face even brighter and perkier than usual. "Abigail! I was starting to worry the cold would keep the two of you indoors."

Grandma smiled. "You know, dear, I actually considered staying home by the fireplace. But I've never missed a hanging before, so here I am, trembling like a mad chihuahua. One of those donuts might warm me right back up."

Sally laughed, her blonde ponytail bouncing around her shoulders. "Sure thing, Grandma. A coffee too, of course. What about you, Abigail?"

"Coffee sounds great, Sally."

"Oh, look!" Grandma gasped just after Sally handed them their drinks. "It's the cow!"

Abigail turned. Someone had wheeled out a life-size cow onto the grassy patch next to the chapel. It looked big, heavy, and surprisingly realistic. Only the red nose and the silver antlers broke the illusion.

One end of a rope had been tied around the cow's middle. The rope ran up to the thin steeple of the chapel and looped back around to fall close to the cow's feet. Lee Lebeau, the town's new lighthouse keeper, and Dag Madsen, caretaker of Wallace Point's historical ship *The Lafayette*, emerged from the crowd. Both were dressed in what seemed to be period-appropriate pirate attire.

Together, they grasped the rope and began to pull. Lee,

who usually preferred to work with plants, seemed to have a bit of a hard time hauling the rope. Lucky for him, Dag had the strength of two men. Abigail saw him cast a glance at Sally, who blushed and turned her attention back to her coffee stand.

Around Abigail, members of the community laughed and cheered, their hands full of hot drinks and sweets. Even Mary Chang, owner of the motel James currently resided at, was in attendance. Her face was as unimpressed as it always was, but Abigail had a feeling the woman was enjoying herself.

Abigail, of course, was enjoying herself immensely despite the cold. This was her first Christmas season in Wallace Point, and so far, the warmth and intimacy were radically different from what she'd experienced in Boston. For probably the millionth time, Abigail was grateful she'd taken the plunge to leave the city life to help Grandma run her small-town store.

The little crowd was so excited and raucous that Abigail almost missed Grandma's words. "They're not here."

"Who's not here, Grandma?"

"Madeline and Hanako. They've never missed a Hanging before. Not that I blame them for missing this year's. What an awful situation."

Abigail thought of Shingo's wife and daughter sitting at their dinner table, an empty place where he ought to be.

Grandma sighed deeply. Her good spirits seemed to seep out of her, and her face looked suddenly tired. "We really ought to do something. Even if that something is a jailbreak."

Abigail studied her grandmother's face. "Grandma? Do you want to go home?"

Grandma nodded slowly. "Yes. Let's go home."

CHAPTER NINE

That night, after Grandma and Missy were tucked away safely in bed, Abigail sat at the kitchen table brooding. She'd never seen Grandma as sad as she was at The Hanging.

Abigail understood and shared Grandma's strong reaction. The two of them had lived long periods of their lives deprived of a family, all because of one person's baseless spite.

Abigail's mother, Sarah, had started out as a good kid, but eventually her self-interest drove a wedge between her and Grandma. Sarah cut her off. Her father followed his little girl, hoping to help her, and eventually died alone.

Even after Abigail was born, her mother refused to let her meet her grandmother. It wasn't until Abigail was an adult and Grandma landed in the hospital that the two finally met.

For years, the two had felt quite alone in the world. Now that they had each other, they wouldn't wish that kind of loneliness on a family as tight-knit as the Yamamotos.

Abigail sighed. Thor rested his big head on her lap, almost falling asleep sitting up as she gave him an ear massage. She held back a laugh as she remembered how terrified Robbie was of the gentle giant. If only he knew what a silly oaf the dog really was.

Would Robbie follow through on setting up a rendezvous with the corrupt officer? Did she even want to meet this guy without some sort of protection?

She thought again of James. He could be intimidating and a good person to have at her side, but he was a hothead. She'd seen him lose his cool before; it wasn't an experience she'd like to repeat any time soon. And, even though he wasn't a cop, Abigail couldn't see James taking too kindly to someone betraying Sheriff Wilson.

Abigail stood, stretched, then walked to the sink to pour herself a glass of water. After downing it, she turned to lean her back against the counter. Thor sat looking up at her, his eyes droopy with sleep.

"I know it's late, Thor," she murmured. "We'll go to bed as soon as I figure this out."

Perhaps figuring this out simply meant laying more pressure on Robbie. He was probably hoping she had forgotten all about him and his half-hearted promise to try to set up a meeting. This evidence-losing cop really could have been the key to exonerating Shingo. Knowing who bought the evidence could lead to the real killer, who was trying to suppress clues.

She whipped out her phone and composed an email:

You working on getting Mr. Butterfingers to agree to a meeting, Ronin-boy?

She hit the send button, flicked the lights off in the kitchen, then headed upstairs to get ready for bed. Giving Robbie a little nudge felt like enough effort for the night.

Robbie responded by the time she had crawled under her covers:

Yeah, but I get to interrogate him with you, right?
  -Lone Ronin

Abigail rolled her eyes. He must've been giddy at the thought of playing a tough guy for once. She flopped onto her stomach and wrote:

Settle down. We're not going to beat the guy up. We're just going to strongly suggest that he come clean lest a little birdie tell Sheriff Wilson what he's been doing. I

---

just need to know who he sold the toy cannon to. Let
him think we're interested in buying the ash and
springs evidence, then we'll spring our trap.

Not a minute later, she received a short and to-the-point
email:

When's a good time for you?
    -Lone Ronin

Abigail released a breath she didn't know she'd been
holding. The fact that Robbie would be able to set up a
meeting so easily was huge. She quickly typed:

The sooner the better.

Just before she drifted off to sleep, she received one more
message from Robbie:

You got it.
    -Lone Ronin

THE NEXT MORNING, Abigail checked her phone as soon as she opened her eyes. There were no other messages from Robbie, and she was sure the day would drag by while she waited for his response.

Luckily, she didn't have much of a chance to feel impatient. Tourists had loved the freebies Grandma set out the night before, and business was booming. There were so many customers coming in and out of the store that Grandma decided to push lunch back an hour or two.

When Abigail finally had a chance to check her phone that afternoon, she saw that Robbie had emailed her an hour before:

He says he'll meet us by the pier tonight. 8 p.m. next to a small yacht called the *Knotty Buoy*. Should I bring protection?

Once again, Abigail caught herself rolling her eyes. Was the guy really thinking about taking a weapon to meet a dirty cop? She could see more customers making their way into the store, so she quickly typed:

Yeah. A warm hat, you bozo. It's going to be cold out

---

there tonight. And just in case I'm not being clear: NO WEAPONS.

As she continued to work and mull over the impending meeting, she took a moment to wonder whether Robbie had a point. Were they walking into actual danger? After all, a cop that black market dealers relied on for "lost" evidence wasn't exactly an upstanding citizen. He might decide Abigail and Robbie needed to take a dive off the pier…

Of course, a weapon wasn't the way to go; that would just escalate a problem. Abigail frowned. They were meeting at the pier, which was dark, and possibly a little secluded, depending on where the *Knotty Buoy* was docked. Maybe there would be passersby or other boat owners, but with the nights as cold as they have been, she doubted anyone else would be strolling around.

Then, Abigail remembered Sally's Book Cafe had a view that looked out over the pier. Bobby Kent, Sally's father, might be Wallace Point's biggest gossip, but Sally was far more reliable.

Abigail hesitated for a second, unsure if she should involve her friend in anything that might be remotely dangerous. After a minute, though, she picked up her phone. Abigail and Robbie needed a safety net in case the situation went south, and Sally would be far enough from the action to be safe herself.

Abigail shot Sally a text asking if she was busy that night.

CHAPTER TEN

Abigail thanked her lucky stars that the evening was a clear one. There wasn't a cloud in the sky to cover the stars, and the moon made everything brighter despite the late hour.

The cold was an obstacle in and of itself. It only stung her cheeks at first, but soon enough, it seeped its way through her layers of coats and sweaters and settled into her skin. Her mouth grew stiff, and even her eyeballs felt frozen over.

Abigail made it to the pier at exactly 7:45. Moving only her frigid eyes, she searched the row of buildings that faced the pier until she found the section that housed the Book Cafe. The window above it was totally dark, for a second, Abigail worried that Sally had forgotten their plan. A moment later lights flicked on briefly before flicking off again. Abigail eased up. That was Sally's way of letting Abigail know she was watching.

Getting Sally on board as her extra pair of eyes hadn't been nearly as difficult as Abigail thought it would be. Sally didn't even ask any questions; she'd simply wanted to know if her involvement would help with a case. When Abigail had assured her it would, Sally jumped at the chance to help.

She'd promised to watch the whole exchange from her place above the Book Cafe. If anything looked suspicious or dangerous, she would call the cops immediately.

"Hey, Silent Night!" hissed a thin voice. Abigail peered into the darkness behind her to see Robbie's scrawny form materialize from the shadows. "You ready for this?"

Abigail sighed. "That was just a dumb screen name I picked to lower your guard."

"Okay. Can I call you Abby? Or Abigail? I already know your name from the police reports."

"Fine, I guess there's really no anonymity in this town anyway. And I prefer Abigail, by the way."

The marina was fairly well-lit, but Robbie and Abigail lingered in the gloom that pooled at the base of the pier. "All right," Abigail began, "let's go find the *Knotty Buoy*."

The yacht was small, mostly white, with edges that swooped and arced in pleasing lines. It sat tied just next to a pool of light provided by the posts along the pier. With a name like the *Knotty Buoy*, Abigail wondered if it belonged to the dirty cop, but decided he wouldn't be dumb enough to meet in front of an expensive toy he might have purchased with his dirty money.

They waited in silence, but not for long.

A tall figure emerged from the darkness at the base of the pier, then walked slowly, steadily along. He slipped from dark to light, light to dark, until finally he edged up to the yacht.

It was an officer from the night of the murder. Abigail recalled James calling him Officer Reynolds. With his large eyes, smooth face, and bold thatch of black hair, Abigail guessed the guy was just a bit younger than James.

"Robbie," he said pleasantly.

Robbie nodded. "Reynolds. This is my associate."

Officer Reynolds stared at Abigail, looking like he was just on the edge of remembering her from a few nights ago. As an officer, he probably saw a lot of faces, so after a moment he shrugged it off. "Evening, miss. Robbie told me you were on the level."

Abigail laughed out a "Yeah," then cleared her throat awkwardly. Just when were they going to spring it on him that this wasn't a business meeting?

An awkward silence fell between the trio, and no one seemed willing to step up and break it. Abigail had the oddest sensation, as if the moment was too surreal for her to process. On one side, she had a sunlight-deprived nerd with an unhealthy obsession for homicide keepsakes; on the other side, she had a young cop who profited from "lost" evidence.

Officer Reynolds didn't care for the silence. He shifted

from one foot to the next, his hands fidgeting visibly in the pockets of his jeans. "So," he said, directing his attention to Robbie. "You had an offer for me? For the... uh... Well, you know."

Abigail raised an eyebrow. She had figured a corrupt cop would be slicker.

Robbie laughed awkwardly and nudged Abigail. "Err, I'll let my associate take the lead on that one."

Officer Reynolds shifted his weight again, squinting at Abigail. "I'm starting to think you look familiar. Do I know you?"

Abigail shrugged, trying to appear nonchalant. "Maybe you've seen me. Everyone's face is familiar in this small town."

"I guess so."

"But I am good friends with Willy and James Wilson."

Officer Reynolds's eyes grew wide, and his baby face flushed crimson. His gaze darted over to Robbie, who again laughed awkwardly. The man shifted his weight once more; this time, he seemed to be considering dashing back down the pier.

"Don't you try anything," Abigail warned. "I got eyes on me, so if you make any moves, you're done for." In her peripheral, she saw Robbie jerk back, but she ignored him.

Officer Reynolds noticed Robbie's surprise. He called her bluff, "Robbie doesn't look so confident."

"That's Robbie for you. As for me, I'm pretty surprised

you're unaware of my reputation. You'll be the fifth person I've landed in jail. That is, if you don't cooperate."

"Listen, it's not what you think. You wouldn't understand. Neither would Willy. I'm not a bad guy. I'm really not."

"Really? So why are you 'losing' and selling evidence? Evidence that could influence an innocent man's case."

Officer Reynolds put his hands out. "That's exactly why I do it! I'm only trying to help."

Abigail's eyebrows shot up. "Care to explain how you're *helping*?"

Officer Reynolds took a moment to regain his composure. "No, I really don't. I haven't said anything you can use anyway. We're done here."

"I want to help Shingo. You say you're helping. How?"

"Look, I help people I know are innocent. That's all I'm doing. I've seen enough guys plant evidence. I'm just trying to balance things out."

"By losing evidence?"

"I'm not confirming or denying anything."

Abigail let the information sink in. "So you're saying there's officers here who are planting evidence?"

"No, no. This was back when I worked in the city." Officer Reynolds shook his head. "When you see that kind of corruption day after day, it takes a toll on you, on your ideals. You go in thinking you'll save the world, or at least your hometown, and that dream just gets sucked out of you. I didn't want to turn hard like all those other guys, so I started taking matters into my own hands. I'm not a bad guy, okay?"

"All right. Then why are you in some small town, pulling the same stunts?"

"I was sick of the city so I transferred to somewhere else, where maybe the force wouldn't need me to clean up its mistakes. But then this guy Shingo gets thrown into hand-cuffs... I live on the same street as him. I see him, his wife, his daughter outside every day. Madeline gives me casseroles because she knows all I have time to make is microwaved junk. Shingo's even helped me fix up my old car. They're a good family. They don't deserve it."

Robbie cleared his throat. Abigail half-wondered whether he had tears in his eyes. "Right on, man," he said. "I know what it's like. The system is broken. As citizens, we've got to fix it however we can. It's our duty."

Abigail wanted to groan. It wasn't that she didn't under-stand where Officer Reynolds was coming from; she did. In fact, she was quite known for taking things into her own hands.

But she wasn't there to condemn or condone Officer Reynolds's actions. She just needed to know one thing. "Who bought the cannon, Officer Reynolds? Because selling the evidence has only muddied things up. Whoever bought it might be trying to hide something."

"It was Guttler. Benjamin Guttler."

"Doesn't ring a bell. Describe him."

"The guy has the most... *notable* potbelly I think I've ever seen."

Mr. Potbelly! Excitement bubbled up in Abigail. This was a guy who had already been acting suspiciously, who had definitely been in attendance the night of the murder, and who Abigail felt she could readily investigate.

Officer Reynolds was looking at her anxiously. "Are you going to say anything to Sheriff Wilson?"

Abigail shook her head. When relief washed over Officer Reynolds's face, she quickly added, "I'm not saying anything for now. But if another piece of evidence goes missing in a future case, I *will* report you. There are other, better ways to make a difference. If that's really what you're trying to do, talk to James. He could use some help with his cold cases."

Despite the frigid air, beads of sweat had gathered along Officer Reynolds's forehead. "I'll do that," he said seriously. There remained nothing else to say, so he nodded and backed off slowly. Just when Abigail was sure he'd fall backwards into the water, he turned around and hurried away.

"Way to go, Abby," Robbie crowed. "You really worked him! Now where do we take this investigation?"

"We? Err, you just return to your battle station and sit tight. I'll let you know when I need your assistance again."

Robbie nodded and gave Abigail a determined salute. "Nice working on the case with you. I'll await your instructions."

After he wandered off, Abigail set out into the cold night.

She had no intentions of working with Robbie any more than necessary, but it was nice to have him on her side.

She was eager to get home, but thinking of Mr. Guttler as a possible suspect helped keep her warm. Why had the guy been so pushy the night of the murder? And why had he been so keen on buying the murder weapon? Was there something about it that might point to him? Abigail could only imagine.

CHAPTER ELEVEN

Breakfast in Grandma's kitchen started out pretty quiet the next morning. Abigail had decided it was too cold to go for a run, and after a quick trip to the yard, Thor agreed. Only Missy still seemed eager to go out.

Without the usual exercise to wake her brain up, Abigail moved in slow motion. She showered slowly, dressed slowly, and ate her oatmeal slowly. She wanted to find a way to get to Mr. Guttler, but her mind was too sluggish that morning.

It wasn't until Grandma, who'd been sitting across the table reading over her oatmeal, threw the daily newspaper in a huff that Abigail finally seemed to crank into gear.

"What is it?" Abigail immediately wondered if Officer Reynolds had fessed up to Sheriff Wilson and the newspaper had somehow caught wind of the story. She really hoped that wasn't the case; now that she thought about it, not reporting evidence theft could land her in hot water too.

"They've identified the body."

"Who was it?"

"His name was Dallas Redford, according to the reporter."

"Oh, they found a replacement for Rachel?"

Grandma peered at the paper. "It appears they did. The new reporter's name is Matthew Hargrove, and according to him, Shingo and Dallas were once roommates in college. Mr. Hargrove says he did some digging and uncovered several complaints Shingo had filed against Dallas way back then."

"Shingo filed against the victim? That's starting to sound like the two had some sort of beef."

"I agree, but these complaints were filed years and years ago. Can a grudge really last that long?" Grandma shook her head. "In these complaints, Shingo claimed that Dallas was copying off his work and stealing his designs."

"Wow, that's pretty bad, college-wise. I once knew someone who was kicked out of college for plagiarizing herself, so stealing someone else's work has to be way worse."

"Well, not really. It seems all the college did was move Dallas to a different floor in the dorm. That's about it."

Abigail put down her spoon and leaned back in her chair. "So, the two men definitely have a connection, and it seems to not be a pleasant one."

"That seems to be the case."

"I think there's more to the story. There has to be. Why

else would Dallas reappear after all these years? Could Dallas have been trying to blackmail Shingo somehow? Or was he there to steal some of his new designs?"

"I think there's more to the story too, but we don't have enough information to start throwing around accusations or theories. We need more facts to work with."

"Yeah, but who do we get them from?"

Grandma took another bite of oatmeal as she mulled it over. "Well, there's Madeline Yamamoto."

"I don't know her very well. Do you?"

"Not very well, no. If you thought Shingo was quiet, you should try to have a conversation with Madeline. She makes the man seem verbose."

"So how do we get her to open up?"

"We've got to show her she can trust us."

Abigail frowned. She doubted Madeline would trust two near-strangers who popped up at her door asking personal questions, even if one of those near-strangers had been Shingo's faithful customer.

Not that she could blame the woman. If a man had mysteriously died in the antique store and everyone suspected Grandma, Abigail would probably ban anyone who tried to come in her front door looking for juicy gossip. How would Madeline know they weren't trying to do the same? Not only that, but Abigail only had a dog to worry about, not a daughter. Hanako was intelligent and extroverted, but she was still a child. Madeline was probably feeling extra protective of her after what happened.

Somewhere in the nooks and crannies of Abigail's mind, an unformed idea stirred. "Hey, Grandma, didn't Hanako mention Camille the night of the murder?"

"Yes!" Grandma's eyes lit up. "Camille is her teacher, or one of them at least—and I'm pretty sure she's close with Madeline."

"I just saw Camille the other day. She basically said she would help in any way she could."

"Abigail, that's perfect! I have her phone number. I'll give her a call and see if she's available this evening after school lets out."

"Sounds like a plan, Grandma," Abigail said. She may not have figured out how to approach Benjamin Guttler, but getting some details from Madeline Yamamoto herself would not be a bad day's work.

THE DAY WAS YET another busy one at Whodunit Antiques. Abigail was on her feet from the moment she flipped the *Open* sign and unlocked the door. Aside from a fifteen-minute break she nabbed over lunch, she didn't get to rest until she locked the door after the last customer.

As she watched the last car drive off, Abigail couldn't help but smile. She was tired, sure, but she wouldn't trade her job for any other in the world. She and Grandma liked to grumble about how crowded it got during the tourist seasons, but there just wasn't anything like helping a customer find a unique piece, telling them the story behind it, and seeing the satisfaction on their faces as they walked out with their treasure and new bit of history.

Still, she didn't hesitate to flop into an overstuffed chair the first moment she could. Grandma was in the kitchen, baking cookies to take to the Yamamotos. Camille had texted that she'd arrive any minute, then the trio would set out together in Abigail's car. The Yamamotos lived at the edge of walking distance from the Lanes, but neither Abigail nor Grandma felt much like undergoing the trek that evening.

Just when Abigail's eyes were drifting shut from exhaustion, a firm knock sounded at the door. Abigail stood up, called over her shoulder to Grandma, and moved quickly to let Camille in from the cold.

Camille's nose was as red as Rudolph's when she wafted inside. She smelled like pencils and crayons and the inner pages of books. "Good afternoon, Abigail."

"Hey, Camille. Grandma's in the kitchen making some of her famous cookies. They're baking now, so it should be safe to step into the kitchen without seeing Grandma's secret recipe…"

In the kitchen, Grandma was just pulling a baking sheet out of the oven. She paused long enough to give Camille a tight squeeze. "Hello, dear. I'm about finished here. In the meantime, you go look around the store. Pick out whatever you want for Hanako."

About ten minutes later, the three women piled into Abigail's car. The sweet smell of fresh-baked cookies filled the small interior. Abigail cranked the heat, and in no time flat, they were as cozy as three mice in a wool sock.

"Is there anything we should know about Madeline before we get there, Camille?" Grandma asked.

"You already know she's pretty shy. She wasn't born and raised here the way Shingo was. I think that's part of why she can be uncomfortable around new people. Don't let that fool you, though. Madeline is probably one of the kindest people I know."

Abigail whistled. "Hanako really won the genetic lottery, didn't she?"

Camille smiled. "I suppose she did, but she isn't taking it for granted. She finishes her work faster than anyone else, and then goes around helping her classmates."

"You know, Abigail," Grandma said, a sly little smirk on her face. "With your wits, you could probably have a kid as sharp as Hanako one day."

Abigail's mouth popped open. "Grandma!"

Camille tried to provide Abigail some backup. "She's in no hurry with life, Granny, and I don't think there's anything wrong with that."

Grandma sighed wistfully. "It's just that I'm getting old. Wouldn't it be a nice bookend to my life to see my beloved granddaughter get married?"

"I already told you, Grandma—you're going to live forever, so stop this talk about bookends."

"I'm still bewildered as to why you're dead-set against James. Perhaps it's because I like him too much. What about

Lee? I know he's a bit on the thin side, but that's nothing we can't fix."

Abigail blinked in disbelief. "This conversation's about to make me crash."

Camille let out a strangled little cough from the backseat. "Turn right here, Abigail. Their house is the last driveway on the left."

Abigail thanked her lucky stars to see that conversation come to such a quick end. She also had a suspicion that Camille was quite smitten with Lee, after the two had bonded over their love of plants at the town's last festival.

The street Abigail turned down was heavily wooded. Other than the Yamamoto house, which they couldn't see from the road, there were only two other houses. Abigail noted a small house with an old car in the driveway. That must've been Officer Reynolds's place, considering he mentioned being neighbors with the Yamamotos and how Shingo helped him fix up the car.

Abigail took the last driveway on the left and followed it up to a two-story house. It looked quite normal. For some reason, she expected something more whimsical, but maybe Shingo saved his creativity for work.

"Well," Grandma said. "Here goes nothing."

When Madeline opened her front door, she saw Camille first, then Grandma and Abigail peeking out from behind her.

"Yes?" Madeline's glossy black hair was pulled into a tight

braid. When she spoke, her hair caught the light from the hallway behind her and gleamed.

"I'm sorry for the surprise, Madeline." Camille's voice was soft, as if she were addressing a skittish deer. "We've brought you and Hanako a few gifts. May we come in?"

Madeline's dark eyes studied the three faces for a moment before she stepped aside to let them through. "Hanako," she called.

As the women followed Madeline into the living room, they heard little footsteps stomp overhead and down the stairs. A second later, Hanako rushed into the room, her face bright and hopeful. When she saw the three women, a little light behind her eyes seemed to blink out. "Oh," she began. "I thought…" Her voice trailed off, only for her to recover a moment later with a big smile as she ran to Camille and threw her arms around her waist.

"I have something for you," Camille said. "Something from Granny Lane's shop of mysteries."

"Something someone made?"

"Yes, something someone made with their own hands a long time ago. Would you like to see what it is?"

Hanako nodded, her eyes bright. Camille pulled a wooden box from her purse and handed it to the girl. She turned it over in her hands a few times, then cranked the knob fixed to the bottom of the box. When she opened the lid, the box played a happy little tune and a bee buzzed lazily around a flower.

Hanako smiled widely. "Cool, a music box!"

Camille laughed. "I thought you'd like it! Granny Lane says we should think of someone's catnip when finding them a gift, and I know how you like automata and bees."

Hanako's eyes widened. "Their catnip?"

Grandma explained, "Something special to that person. Something they collect or enjoy."

In quick succession, she wrapped her little arms around Camille's waist, Abigail's, then Grandma's. "Thank you! I'm going to add this bee to my collection!" She then turned and darted back up the stairs.

Madeline was silent for a moment before saying, "Thank you for that thoughtful gift. She hasn't been herself."

"And with good reason," Camille murmured. "How are *you* doing, Madeline?"

"I miss Shingo," Madeline said simply. "Please, follow me to the kitchen. I'll make everyone some tea."

They followed Madeline and settled around the dining room table. Abigail soaked in everything around her, hoping to absorb an important clue by osmosis.

The house was different from Grandma's Victorian home that burst at the seams with memories and antiques. In general, this house had far fewer things: less furniture, hardly any art hanging from the walls, and little décor. Abigail had expected to see tools and half-finished oddities in every corner, not rooms that were nearly bare. In its own way, though, the emptiness was soothing.

"You have a beautiful home," she said.

"Thank you." Madeline filled a ceramic kettle with water

and set it onto the stove. "Shingo and I have always felt that home is sacred. It should be a safe haven, where one can always find tranquility, love, and a quiet corner."

Madeline took a stack of small ceramic plates from a cupboard and placed it on the table with a neat pile of cloth napkins. After she fetched mugs and brought those to the table as well, she paused. "It doesn't feel the same without him here."

Grandma put a cookie on everyone's plate, then raised hers. "Here's to hoping he comes home soon. What happened to him is just awful."

Madeline bowed her head briefly. "Thank you, Mrs. Lane. Sadly, not everyone agrees with you."

"What do you mean? And feel free to call me Granny."

"Yes, Granny. I mean that many people seem to suspect Shingo of this terrible thing. But he didn't do it. I refuse to believe he did it."

"So do we, dear. Now listen, I know that you probably don't want to talk about the past, and I know you've probably told the police everything you can think of. But Abigail and I would like to dig a bit deeper to find anything that might prove Shingo's innocence. Will you help us?"

The kettle began to sing, and Madeline moved back to the stove. She turned off the heat and poured the boiling water into a kettle already prepped with tea leaves. She brought the kettle to the table, poured everyone a cup, and finally took a seat.

Madeline looked from one to the other. "I know you've

solved two murders so far. With your track record, all I can ask is, what would you like to know?"

Relief washed over Abigail but she didn't let it show. Grandma was keeping her poker face on too. "We read about Dallas Redford in the paper this morning. Can you tell us anything more about him?"

"The paper only covered a small hint of Shingo's relationship with Dallas. They missed a lot."

Abigail leaned forward. "Like what?"

"After Dallas was moved to a different floor in the dorm, Shingo thought he'd finally have some peace to work. But he didn't. Dallas continued to antagonize him."

"Why?" Abigail asked. "Why was Dallas so... obsessed with Shingo?"

Madeline shook her head. "I think at first Dallas really looked up to Shingo. His focus was on machines, while Shingo's was on clockwork automata, but he saw Shingo almost as a mentor. He began to incorporate a lot of Shingo's designs into his own devices. In time, he convinced himself that those ideas were really his own, that he had the superior engineering mind."

"I've seen that before in children," Camille chimed in. "In some cases, it can be downright eerie. You can show the child all the evidence in the world that the red truck never belonged to him, and he will continue to insist that it has always been his. He so badly wants the truck that his mind obliges and tweaks his perception of reality."

Madeline nodded emphatically. "Dallas was just like that.

It came to a point where he really pushed Shingo to the edge. Shingo did everything he could to put a stop to the harassment, but he had little success."

Abigail frowned. "What about the school? They never took serious action against Dallas?"

"No." For a moment, Madeline's voice was tinged with bitterness. "Dallas's parents were wealthy alumni. At one point, Shingo even had evidence that Dallas broke into his room. He took it to the dean. All Dallas's parents had to do was make a generous donation, and Shingo's complaint was swept under the rug."

"That's an outrage," Grandma said. Abigail glanced at her and saw the woman wasn't kidding. Her usually rosy cheeks were livid with indignation.

Madeline fiddled with the napkin in her hands. "After that, Shingo started getting paranoid. He didn't feel safe or supported. He stopped sleeping. He even stopped talking to me for a few months."

"That's pretty intense." Abigail took a moment to sip at her steaming tea. "How was everything resolved?"

"Dallas transferred to a different college."

Grandma tilted her head. "Why? After everything he got away with, why would he just up and leave?"

"To be honest, Granny, I don't know. I think it was entirely his decision."

Abigail rubbed at the rim of her teacup. Dallas had apparently been more than a nuisance to Shingo in the past. And after having gone the legal route and been ignored, she could understand why Shingo might consider taking matters into his own hands. But there was one obvious problem. "Why now? Why would Dallas show up now, after all of these years? And would Shingo have held a grudge for that long?"

For the first time since Abigail had met her, an amused smile graced Madeline's face. It made her pretty face even more pleasant. But the smile faded too soon. "Shingo would never hold a grudge like that. It doesn't make any sense. Shingo hasn't so much as mentioned Dallas in over a decade. I thought it was all in the past. In fact, I'd just about forgotten all about it."

Grandma frowned. "Could Dallas have been harassing Shingo again? Maybe his life didn't turn out the way he'd expected, and he decided to blame an old rival rather than face himself."

"I don't think so. If Dallas had reappeared in Shingo's life, he would have told me. He tells me everything."

Abigail thought that over. Madeline and Shingo seemed incredibly close. Could he have kept Dallas's reappearance a secret from his wife? And if so, why?

Camille stacked the ceramic plates, now dusted with cookie crumbs, and carried them to the kitchen sink. When she returned, she said gently, "It's a school night. I should really be going."

Grandma and Abigail were already pushing themselves to their feet. Madeline walked them to the door and thanked them each sincerely for visiting. Just as they were about to walk out, she spoke up one more time. "I know Shingo didn't do this. I know it for a fact. That toy cannon and automaton couldn't have been made by him."

Abigail was all ears. "How do you know that, Madeline?"

"There were leftover screws in the ashes, according to the papers. He never uses screws, or any other metal for that matter; only wood. His sole exception is springs. It's a point of pride for him."

Grandma listened intently. "Thank you for that. We can't make any promises, of course, but Abigail and I will do our best to get to the bottom of this."

They thanked her again, scurried to the car, and cranked up the heat. As Abigail reversed down the driveway, she heard Grandma muttering to herself.

"What was that, Grandma?"

Grandma glared through her window at the houses bedecked with Christmas lights. "The Yamamotos have been failed left and right. First, that ridiculous institution failed to protect Shingo from Dallas Redford. Then, poor Shingo was wrongly arrested for murdering his aggressor. And now, our community has left Madeline and Hanako high and dry. You know, I didn't see a single casserole dish in her fridge! No one has brought her any. You better believe I'm going to fix this right up."

"Wait, back up. When did you look in her fridge?"

"I have my ways, Abigail. Besides, that's not the point. The point is that Madeline hasn't received a single casserole. What is Wallace Point coming to? Just wait until I get a hold of the Granny Gang."

CHAPTER TWELVE

After they dropped off Camille and made it back home, Grandma immediately picked up the phone and started making calls. Pretty soon, she had extracted casserole commitments from over half of the Granny Gang.

When she felt she'd recruited enough cohorts, Grandma started banging pots and pans together in the kitchen. Abigail trailed her absently, peering over Grandma's shoulder as she cut butter into a skillet, and shaped ground beef into patties. Finally, Grandma ran out of patience.

"Abigail, dear, you're making me feel like I've got a tail attached to my rump. What's on your mind?"

"What?" Abigail said, picking up a potato and then dropping it on the floor. Grandma whacked the back of Abigail's hand with a wooden spoon. "Ow!"

Grandma smiled sweetly. "I was just saying you seem preoccupied. What's on your mind?"

Abigail picked up the potato and washed it off. "Okay, I've got something on my mind, but you have to promise not to ask about my sources."

"Your sources, huh?" Grandma arched an eyebrow. "Fine, I won't ask."

"Word on the street is that Mr. Potbelly bought the 'missing' toy cannon."

"What? You know who stole the cannon?"

"I didn't say that. I said there's a rumor going around that Mr. Potbelly bought it."

Grandma put a hand on her hip. "That ought to be reported to the police, don't you think?"

"Well, it hasn't been confirmed. It's just something I heard from one of my sketchier sources. But I think the guy might be worth looking into."

"The nerve of some people," Grandma said, shaking her head. She turned back to the stove. "Buying a murder weapon, and for what? To flip it for a profit later? There could be crucial fingerprints on that cannon!"

"Yeah, that's what I was thinking."

"We need to find him before he skips town."

"But how?"

"We go downtown and ask around, of course. I'll just pack all of this up in the fridge, and we'll get going!"

As much as Abigail could use a good meal right now, she forced a smile and said, "Great!"

Her stomach growled in protest.

THEY MADE a beeline for Sally's Book Cafe. It was just hitting 8:00 p.m. when they arrived and Sally was in the process of closing up shop. Grandma had to rap on the door to get her attention.

Sally bounced over and unlocked the door to let them in. "Well, hello! To what do I owe this pleasure?"

Abigail hugged her friend, suppressing a giggle as Sally wriggled in her arms. Sally was the most energetic and friendly person she'd ever met. No wonder she had trouble staying still, even for a hug.

"We came to ask you some questions, dear, if you don't mind."

Sally's face was a perfect mask of surprise. "Am I in trouble?"

"Why no, of course not," Grandma cackled. "You just might have the information we're looking for."

"Come right on in then, take a seat. Do you mind if I mop while you ask questions?"

Grandma settled into an overstuffed armchair while Abigail fetched a second mop to help Sally. "We're wondering if you've seen a man in here," Grandma began. "He's a collector who came into town, ostensibly, to attend Shingo's re-opening."

"Oh. My. Goodness." Sally's blonde hair whipped around

her shoulders. "Does this gentleman have a particularly prominent gut?"

"We call him Mr. Potbelly," Abigail offered.

"I know exactly who you're talking about. His name is Mr. Guttler, but Mr. Potbelly suits him too. That man!"

"What has he done?" Grandma eagerly leaned forward in her chair.

"Nothing terrible, really, but he is such a nuisance. He comes in here every day harassing my customers. He's looking for locals, but they know to stay away during tourist season. I've had to ask him multiple times to stop accosting my clients. He always buys so many pastries too. I suppose I should be happy about that, but he hardly leaves anything for anybody else."

Abigail wrung out her mop. "What does he want?"

"He's going all around town trying to buy rare Shingo originals from us residents. Poor Piper had to call the police to get the man off her property. No one trusts him; we're all pretty sure he's just trying to profit off the latest murder."

With the mopping done, Sally dumped the dirty water and set everything back neatly. Grandma stood, and Abigail moved toward the door.

"One more question, dear. Do you happen to know where this gentleman is staying?"

Sally squeezed her eyes shut while she thought. After a minute, she shook her head. "Nope, no idea."

"Well, thank you. You've been a tremendous help."

Once outside, they made a run for the car in order to

escape the cold air. Abigail was the faster of the two by far, opening Grandma's door before running around to the driver's side and jumping in. Though they'd been inside less than ten minutes, the car already felt like Alaska.

"He's quite elusive for a guy with a potbelly," Abigail muttered once Grandma was safely seated. "He doesn't sound like the type anyone would tolerate for free, so he's gotta be staying at either a hotel or a bed and breakfast. Can't we narrow those down?"

Grandma grinned. "Good point. There are only two places he could be. He's either staying at Mary Chang's motel, or at the bed and breakfast on Main Street. But it's getting a bit late and we haven't even had dinner yet. Let's call it a day for now."

"Yeah, I guess. It just feels like we're almost on top of him."

"Think about it this way. The man has been knocking on doors for days. Soon he'll make his way to our neighborhood. If we don't find him, he'll find us. He knows I have quite the collection of Shingo creations. It's just a matter of him gathering up the courage to ask."

"True," Abigail mused. "All right, we'll take a break for the night then. I'll ask James tomorrow morning whether he's seen Mr. Potbelly at the motel."

Abigail pulled out of her parking space and headed for home, dreaming of a hot fire, a hefty burger, and a big, warm Thor.

CHAPTER THIRTEEN

Abigail pulled into the parking lot of Mary Chang's motel bright and early the following morning. The motel sat at the edge of Wallace Point, and just a few short months before, it had been the scene of a murder. Now, James had made the place his headquarters.

She'd texted him the night before about meeting up to talk, which led to him inviting her over for a continental breakfast. So there she was, her car still mostly covered with frost. She figured she could keep an eye out for Benjamin Guttler, pick James's brain, and have a decent excuse not to go on a run on such a chilly morning.

Hurrying inside, she walked through the lobby and into the dining room. The dining room contained half a dozen tables. Alongside one wall, a table boasted a literal cornucopia stuffed with a variety of breads. Cheeses and fresh fruits crowded around the display, and large pitchers of coffee brought it all together.

"Not bad, huh, Cupcake?" James said from behind her.

Abigail turned to see his usual frumpy self. "Not bad at all. I didn't know motels had continental breakfasts."

"I'm not sure they do. But this is a hotel now, according to Miss Chang. She told me 'motel' is too catchy when you combine it with the word 'murder.'"

Abigail laughed. "Oh, as in 'Murder Motel'? Yeah, I can see why she'd try to disassociate her business with what happened a few months ago."

"Just don't tell her that 'Homicide Hotel' is also pretty catchy. Go ahead and load up. My table's over this way."

"You have your very own table?"

"More or less. I'm kind of a regular here, these days. It's where I talk to most of my clients."

Abigail took a plate and picked out a bit of everything before following James to a table by the window. The table offered a clear view of the dining room and the window looked out over the parking lot.

Once seated, Abigail took a closer look around her. The carpet had been replaced, the tables and chairs looked nearly new, and the smell of fresh paint still seemed to linger in certain corners. "Mary Chang has really done a number on this place, hasn't she?"

"That woman is a force of nature. She's doing all the

renovations herself, and she refuses help—even free help."
Mary walked in just then, so James lowered his voice. "We've
worked out a pretty good deal, she and I. She lets me rent the
room on a monthly basis for cheap, and all I gotta do is keep
an eye on things and report any funny business."

"That's right!" Mary snapped as she replenished the
cornucopia. "I will not have any more crime in my hotel. You
heard that? *Hotel.* This is no longer 'The Roach Motel' or
'The Murder Motel.' No more killing in my place of business.
Except if I hear someone call my business anything other
than The Seaside Hotel. Then maybe I will murder someone.
But only *I* get to kill someone in *my* hotel!"

Abigail threw her head back and laughed again. "Don't
worry, Miss Chang, I doubt anyone would dare defy you. But
I do have to ask... Isn't calling this place The Seaside Hotel
false advertising? The whole thing is surrounded by a forest."

Mary's eyes narrowed. "If you climb one of the trees, you
can see the sea. Close enough!"

Abigail and James started in on their breakfast, but were
interrupted several times by a handful of other hotel guests.
They all greeted James by name, asked after his father, and
introduced themselves to Abigail.

"You're Mr. Popularity around here, aren't you?" Abigail
teased after their latest visitor drifted off to the breakfast
spread.

"You know, you're about the only person in Wallace Point
who doesn't find me thoroughly charming."

Abigail smirked. "That's because I know you so well, James."

"Very funny. Really, though, I'm not the only extended-stay guest here. After a while, you become neighbors."

"You seem pretty fond of The Seaside Hotel."

"I am. In fact, I think it's a perfect place to set up a PI office."

Abigail looked up, surprised. When James had told her he was moving into the hotel, he indicated he'd stay for a few months before heading back to his life and PI business back in the city. "Are you planning on making your stay more permanent?"

"Yeah, actually." James's gaze grew soft and faraway. "I'm starting to wonder why I ever left in the first place. Anyway, I suppose we better get down to business. Anything to report?"

Abigail considered her words carefully before speaking. She didn't need James turning in her sources, which he almost certainly would do if he knew about what Officer Reynolds had been doing all this time. "Well, there's this guy who's an avid collector of Shingo's creations. Some people are saying he might be *too* avid."

James nodded. "I know the guy. My dad's had a couple of people complain about him. I think some of the boys even had to drive out to Piper's house to escort him off the property. By the time they got there, though, he'd driven off. My guess is Piper threatened him with a musket."

"Sounds like her. What do you know about him?"

"Not much, just that he's here for Shingo's automata. Once he knows someone has a rare piece, he just won't take no for an answer."

"Yeah, I'm definitely suspicious about the guy. His timing, his behavior, all of it just seems a little… I don't know… off. Do you know where he's staying?"

"No, but I can tell you he's not staying here."

Abigail took a bite of her croissant. If Guttler had been staying at The Seaside Hotel, she figured the guy would have come down to breakfast, so she didn't doubt James for a second. "Do you think he might have something to do with the case?"

"No. I'm thinking he's just an opportunist. Probably thinks his collection is going to be worth a whole lot more once Shingo's found guilty of murder."

"Once he's found guilty? Not *if*?"

James's shoulders sagged. "I mean, Shingo hasn't denied his guilt yet. That worries me."

"That doesn't automatically make him guilty, though."

"Right, but it doesn't help his case either." James looked so downcast that Abigail almost wanted to give his shoulder a reassuring squeeze. Sure, he hadn't known Shingo very well, but James had looked up to him. Shingo's toy store seemed to have been a big part of James's life before his mother's tragic passing. Abigail wondered whether losing Shingo made James feel like he'd lost another fragment of his already tattered childhood.

Abigail finished her meal feeling a new sense of resolve.

Shingo was an important thread in the fabric of the Wallace Point community. She had to get to the bottom of this case for Shingo, for his family, and for the town she so dearly loved.

CHAPTER FOURTEEN

When Abigail made it home from her breakfast with James, there were already a handful of customers waiting on the front porch. They stamped their feet and pulled their hats tight over their ears, but apparently not one of them wanted to give up their place for the warmth of a car heater.

By the time Abigail parked and climbed up the porch steps, Grandma was unlocking the door. When the customers heard the doorknob rattle, they pressed closer to the door like a pack of lurking wolves. They even eyed Abigail warily to see if she would try to cut to the front of the loose line. Tourists most definitely, otherwise they would have known Abigail wasn't a threat.

Grandma swung the door open and, in her best

disarming old lady voice, exclaimed, "Good morning, young-sters! And welcome to Whodunit Antiques! Come on in here, before you turn into icicles!"

She stood aside as the tourists filed in. Abigail brought up the rear with a grin, and spoke loud enough for the whole store to hear. "Are those fresh-baked cookies I smell?"

"Only my ultra-famous cookies," Grandma said just as loudly. "I whipped them up using my super-secret cookie recipe."

Abigail knew more about the secret recipe than Grandma was comfortable with. In fact, most of Wallace Point knew Grandma's "secret recipe," which featured a visit to the refrigerated section in the grocery store as a key ingredient. But Grandma didn't know she knew, and the tourists didn't know anything at all, so why spoil the fun?

"Isn't it too early in the morning for cookies, Grandma?" Abigail continued.

"It's never too early for hot, fresh-from-the-oven cookies on a freezing morning. Besides, it's almost Christmas!" Grandma winked at Abigail, then asked, quietly, "Any news from James?"

"Not much, other than the fact that Mr. Potbelly is defi-nitely not staying at the Seaside Hotel."

"The Seaside Hotel? Now, where in the world is that?"

"Mary is renovating and rebranding. She doesn't ever want to hear the words 'Murder Motel' again."

"But you can't even see the ocean from there."

"That's what I said, but it seems once Mary insists on

something, nobody dares to question her. Anyway, some good news for you and the rest of the town: James might make his stay here more permanent."

"More permanent, huh?" Grandma's eyes twinkled.

Abigail sighed. "Anyway, Mr. Guttler must be staying in that bed and breakfast downtown. Maybe we should pay him a visit this evening."

"Sounds like a plan to me, dear. But first, let's help these tourists lighten their pockets."

THE DAY WAS JUST as busy as the ones before it. It was exhausting, but Abigail didn't mind. She met a retired couple who lived out of their vintage Airstream and traveled all over the American continent. She also helped a young woman pick out vintage jewelry for her great grandmother, who, at the age of 101, still walked a mile a day and lived on her own.

Abigail loved having the dogs underfoot, and she loved working with her grandmother. The woman was an exceptional salesperson with a knack for finding something a customer really wanted, even if she didn't have the exact piece they were originally looking for. She had tons of information stored up in her head, which resulted in every customer leaving with a world of knowledge about their newly acquired antique.

A bit before closing time, the bell above the door chimed,

and a fresh draft of cold air swept into the room. Abigail, who was wandering around the store helping customers and tidying up, glanced toward the entry and froze.

There stood the elusive Mr. Potbelly, a hungry look in his coal-black eyes. The man had round cheeks and a round head topped by a vintage top hat. His nose was long and sharp, his small lips swept toward one side of his face in a crooked smile, and his neck was practically nonexistent under his striped scarf. Now that she was getting a good long look at Benjamin Guttler, she thought he resembled a snowman.

"Florence Lane!" boomed the man into the quiet store. Abigail noticed a couple of customers jump in surprise. "Florence Lane, I'm here for that blasted nutcracker!"

Abigail started toward Mr. Guttler, but Grandma was way ahead of her.

"Mr. Guttler," Grandma called from behind the cash register, where she was wrapping a set of bone china for a customer. "Please keep your voice down in my store. If you would like my assistance, you may approach me like a civilized person."

Mr. Guttler chuckled in good humor as he strode toward Grandma. He leaned against the check-out counter and helped himself to the plate of cookies Grandma had set there just a few minutes before.

"You know the rules about my cookies, don't you, Mr. Guttler?"

"You eat something, you buy something," Mr. Guttler boomed just as loudly as before. He chuckled again, and his whole belly trembled. "I could never forget your cookies, Florence, or you... or that little old nutcracker you've got hidden away in here. I'll eat this cookie, buy that nutcracker, and I'll be right on my way."

Grandma finished packaging the china and sent her customer off with a smile that was at once warm, apologetic, and good-natured. Still lingering by the antique quilts, Abigail was pretty impressed by how cool Grandma was managing to stay.

"I told you years ago, Mr. Guttler, and I'm telling you now: I'm not selling it."

"I must say, Florence, I'm pleasantly surprised you remember my name. I, too, have thought of you fondly after all these years."

"Your name is burned into my memory whether I like it or not. It has nothing to do with fondness."

"I'll pay you $10,000 for that nutcracker."

Abigail's stomach dropped. Then, when it had gone as far as it could go, it flew up to her throat. She lowered herself as subtly as she could into a nearby chair.

Grandma, though, didn't miss a beat. "I didn't sell it to you for $500 back then, and I won't sell it to you for $10,000 now. Why would you even pay that much?"

"Let's just say I have a feeling the value of Shingo's automata is about to skyrocket." Benjamin Guttler bit into another cookie. "I mean, who wouldn't want an automaton made by a madman?"

"Okay," Grandma said suddenly.

"Okay? Okay what?"

"Okay, I'll sell it to you."

Abigail's jaw dropped. She closed it again quickly, knowing better than to doubt her grandmother. Still, what was Grandma doing?

Benjamin Guttler couldn't contain his excitement. He hopped from one foot to the other. "Wonderful, Florence, wonderful. Name your price."

"Your right sock."

Even Benjamin Guttler paused at that. "My right sock? For a Shingo Yamamoto vintage original?"

"Do you want it or not?"

Abigail couldn't believe what she was hearing. Her stomach, now back in its normal location, twisted queasily. Was this an early warning sign of senility? Was Abigail going to have to intervene?

"All right," Mr. Guttler said, shaking his round head. "If that's what you want, I'm not going to judge. As long as I get that nutcracker."

"Yes, yes. Just give me the sock first."

Chuckling, Mr. Guttler looked around for a chair, plopped down, then whipped off his right shoe, followed by his right sock. He slipped the shoe back on and presented the sock to Grandma with a deep bow. Curiously, his top hat remained affixed on his head. "One right sock, as you requested."

Once the sock was firmly in Grandma's hand, a sly smile crept across her face. "Good. Now, I regret to tell you this, but you're officially banned from my store."

Mr. Guttler frowned. "You're banning me?"

"That's right. Abigail and I," Grandma nodded at Abigail, "we reserve the right to ban anyone we please from the store. And you, Mr. Guttler, with your brash and unyielding ways, have lost the privilege of shopping at my fine establishment."

"I guess I can't argue with that," Mr. Guttler said, although to Abigail's ears, it sounded like he very much wanted to argue with Grandma. "But why steal my sock? It's rather unpleasant to be missing a sock in this weather, you know."

"Thor," Grandma called. Her tone was authoritative, stern, and Thor immediately loped over to her, Missy trotting at his heels. Grandma brought the sock down so the dogs could smell it, then she handed the sock back to Mr. Guttler. "I was only borrowing it. Now that the store guard dogs know your scent, they will rip you to shreds if they catch so much as a whiff of you in this store again. Isn't that right, Thor and Missy?"

Thor, as if he really had been trained to rip banned customers to shreds, growled menacingly. Missy yipped.

Mr. Guttler groaned, all of his ingratiating good humor melting away. "I think it's about time someone retired you to a nursing home, lady."

That was more than enough for Abigail. She jumped out of her seat and strode toward Mr. Guttler. Her manner was brusque, causing Thor's short hair to stand on end as he picked up her mood. "You heard her, sir. Get out before I feed you to Thor."

"All right, all right." Mr. Guttler backed away from the counter, taking one more of Grandma's cookies with him. "Apparently, you're as crazy as she is. I offered you $10,000, for goodness' sake. What's wrong with you people?"

"Thor," Abigail growled, and the big dog growled too, taking a step toward the retreating man. That was enough for Benjamin Guttler. His round face turned quite white and he lost no more time finding the door.

Grandma turned to Abigail once the dust settled. "Did you like that trick with the sock?"

"Yeah. Although at first I thought you had lost your mind."

"No matter. I think we finally have confirmed a motive."

"Oh?"

"He has a large collection, perhaps the most complete collection anyone has. If Shingo is found guilty of murder, the value of that collection will skyrocket. The man offered me $10,000 for a single nutcracker. That's a tad suspicious, don't you think?"

"When you put it that way, Grandma, yeah, definitely." Abigail glanced around the store. All the other customers had disappeared during Mr. Guttler's boisterous discussion. The store was empty and closing time was fast approaching.

Outside, Mr. Guttler's engine roared to life. "Hey, Grandma. James taught me a little bit about trailing people. Why don't we see what this guy's up to?"

Grandma smirked, adventure in her eyes. "Yes, why don't we?"

CHAPTER FIFTEEN

Grandma insisted on taking her pink golf cart, claiming it was the perfect vehicle for their stealthy task. She also insisted on taking binoculars and steaming thermoses of instant hot cocoa. Lucky for them, Mr. Guttler didn't get very far by the time they made it outside.

"It'd be nice if one of us had an inconspicuous vehicle," Abigail said, thinking of her VW Bug. "It won't be long before he notices us."

Grandma revved the golf cart's engine, though it didn't make much noise, being electric. "Have you noticed the dozens of golf carts that roam the streets of Wallace Point on a daily basis? We're just part of the Wallace Point scenery."

Abigail thought of the Granny Gang. Each had her own tricked-out golf cart, and most of them made Grandma's look tame. "I guess that's true."

The golf cart might indeed have been their stealthiest choice, but it certainly wasn't their warmest. Even after Grandma zipped up the weather-resistant fabric panels, the cold air seeped in and numbed their noses. Abigail was grateful for the hot cocoa in her hands.

For a second, she worried that they had already lost the trail. Luckily, though, they weren't too far behind Benjamin Guttler, and he wasn't moving very quickly. The man had parked his car on the street, not too far from Whodunit Antiques, and now he was on foot. He went up to a house and knocked on the door.

"Does he know them?" Abigail asked.

"Maybe, but I doubt it."

Someone answered the door and had a brief conversation with Mr. Guttler. Soon the conversation ended, and Mr. Guttler walked down the driveway, along the sidewalk, and up the driveway to the house next door. He knocked again.

Abigail shook her head. "No way. Is he literally walking door to door? Is he really asking every single resident of Wallace Point to sell their Shingo originals to him?"

"It sure seems that way. And, really, it makes sense."

"How's that?"

"Well, Wallace Point would be *the* place to sift for rarer, uncatalogued automata by Shingo. I know for a fact he gifted many of his earlier pieces to people around town when he was just starting out."

"This guy is unreal. Trying to profit off such an awful event. Does he even care that Shingo might be innocent?"

Grandma shrugged. "I don't think he's thinking about Shingo at all. Just his own wallet."

The next door that Mr. Guttler knocked on was Camille Bellerose's. Grandma thrust the binoculars into Abigail's lap. "Watch and report."

Abigail brought the binoculars to her eyes. The image through the lenses tilted and swung wildly while she found Mr. Guttler. Adjusting the view, she could see that Camille had just opened the door.

"They're talking. Seems like Camille's asking him what he wants. He's talking… Oh, man, she doesn't look happy. Yeesh, I think she's yelling at the guy now. But… But I guess he's not taking the hint? She's pointing now. She must be telling him to get off her property. He's still staying put. She disappeared."

"Disappeared?" Grandma echoed, clutching the arm of Abigail's coat.

"Wait," Abigail continued. "She's back. Oh! She's holding a tomato the size of a cantaloupe! How is she even growing tomatoes in winter? He's still not budging. Whoa!"

"What? What is it, Abigail?"

"She threw the tomato at his face," she answered, her voice filled with admiration. "She actually threw that tomato at him."

Grandma took the binoculars and peered through. After a moment, she started to cackle. "Oh, goodness. Benjamin Guttler is drenched in tomato!"

The binoculars were no longer necessary. With their

naked eyes, they could see Guttler spin on his heel and storm back down Camille's driveway. Instead of moving on to the next house, he stalked down the street toward his car.

"I bet he's going back to the bed and breakfast. He's not done with this neighborhood, though. That's my guess."

Abigail shook her head. "This guy is ridiculously persistent."

"Maybe *too* persistent. If he really did have anything to do with the murder, I don't think he would be so bold."

"Yeah," Abigail sighed. "I'm starting to think the same thing."

Grandma checked her wristwatch. "I'm not ready to give up on Mr. Guttler. It's almost six. The bed and breakfast should be serving dinner soon. Think he might partake?"

"I've no doubt. Did you see how many of your cookies he ate?"

"Five," Grandma said dryly.

"Yeah. He doesn't seem like the type to skip a meal."

Grandma grinned wickedly. "How about we provide him some company while he eats? Somebody this obsessed with Shingo's automata might know a vital clue."

Abigail nodded eagerly, hoping Grandma was on to something.

CHAPTER SIXTEEN

T he extreme cold persuaded them to stop back at the store; stealth was no longer a priority, so Abigail's Bug with the powerful heater would do just fine.

Though they were in a bit of a hurry, they couldn't help but croon over all of the Christmas decor they passed. Pretty much every house in Wallace Point was festooned with glowing reindeer and blow-up Santa Clauses. The multitudes of little Christmas lights were so bright that streetlights were no longer necessary.

The bed and breakfast was no exception. It looked like a gingerbread house straight out of a fairy tale. Giant candy canes lined the walk up to the main door. Enormous stars with long tails swooped through the bare trees, and icicle lights dripped from the eaves. Abigail almost wished she had a pair of sunglasses, the lights were so bright.

Inside, Abigail and Grandma settled onto a bench in the lobby. The bench had an excellent view of the dining room, and they were just in time to see Mr. Guttler choose a table and sit down.

He wore a different set of clothes, and his face looked shiny and flushed, as if he'd just scrubbed it vigorously with cold water. Despite his fresh appearance, Mr. Guttler's face betrayed his grumpiness.

"I guess he didn't enjoy Camille's home-grown produce," Grandma snickered.

A waiter approached Mr. Guttler, and the man's round face instantly brightened. He opened his menu and pointed at it.

"Let's move in when the waiter leaves," Abigail suggested. "That'll make him our captive audience, because there's no way he'll pass up on his meal."

Grandma nodded her agreement, and they both moved to the edge of the bench, ready to jump up at any moment.

They had to wait a while. Mr. Guttler continued to point to several more things before finally relinquishing his menu to the dazed waiter.

"Let's go," Grandma said.

The two Lane women got up from their little bench, strode across the room, and eased into the empty seats at Mr. Guttler's table. The man looked up and jumped.

"You've been a busy boy," Abigail noted.

Grandma added, "Seems you've worked up an appetite, knocking on so many doors."

Mr. Guttler groaned. His eyebrows bunched together and his coal-black eyes dimmed. "Why is everyone in town treating me like I'm some miscreant? I'm merely a collector!"

He looked so downcast that Abigail almost felt sorry for him. But then she remembered his motive. "Maybe because you're trying to profit off a Wallace Point resident's misfortune? And don't act so innocent, Mr. Guttler. I know you purchased the cannon that killed Mr. Redford, which was stolen from the police evidence room."

Mr. Guttler paled, then grunted. He opened his mouth to say something, but the waiter came by just then with a basket of biscuits. He tore his first biscuit in half and spread butter liberally over it while the waiter offered menus to Abigail and Grandma. Once they'd declined and the server had moved away again, Mr. Guttler stuffed a bite of biscuit into his mouth.

"I'm not trying to profit off anyone," he began with his mouth full. "And I admit, I've been having second thoughts about that cannon purchase."

"How do you even have those kinds of connections, anyway?"

"I don't! I was just going door to door, and what do you know? I meet a fellow willing to sell me the cannon! But now I'm starting to think I shouldn't have done that."

Abigail's eyes narrowed. "Yeah, you think? Are you going to make things right or am I going to have to make an anonymous tip?"

"Oh, err, yes. In fact, I'll return the cannon to the station after dinner, albeit anonymously." Mr. Guttler wiped the corner of his mouth with the back of his hand and continued, "Please don't think ill of me. I'm simply trying to build the most complete collection of Shingo's works. I've been working on it for years. But now I've got a hunch that if he's found guilty, a bunch of vultures will come out of the woodwork, buying his automata just to turn a profit."

Abigail asked, "We're glad you're choosing to return the cannon. So, you're *just* completing your collection? With absolutely no intention to sell it for a pretty penny?"

"Exactly! Can't I just be an admirer of Shingo's work?"

"Maybe." Grandma shrugged. "But if you want to convince me, I need you to give me something."

Benjamin Guttler frowned. "What? My left sock?"

"A lead."

"A lead?"

"Yes. Is there anything about the details of the case that aren't adding up for you? I'm sure you've read the papers."

"I have." Mr. Guttler nodded. "And, actually, now that you mention it—"

But before he could elaborate, three waiters approached with his orders. Mr. Guttler seemed to entirely forget the conversation at hand; he was too busy inhaling the aromas from all the plates.

Mr. Guttler dove happily into his meal. "Just push those plates they set in front of you to the middle of the table. I'll get around to them shortly."

Abigail was on the edge of her seat. "You were saying...?" she pressed.

Mr. Guttler nodded and opened his mouth. Instead of responding though, he took a big bite out of a chicken leg. The meat looked like it had been barbecued to perfection, and with Mr. Guttler enjoying it so much, Abigail was starting to get hungry.

"Well, out with it!" Grandma exclaimed. She only had one thing on her mind, and no amount of barbecue was going to make her forget it. "An innocent man is in jail!"

"Florence, Florence, you must be patient! My blood sugar was getting dangerously low." Mr. Guttler grabbed a handful of sugar packets, ripped the tops off them in one movement, and dumped the white granules into a glass of iced tea. Abigail grimaced as he gulped the beverage down.

Finally, Mr. Guttler finished his thought. "All right, ladies, here's the one thing that doesn't make sense to me. The paper says that the murder weapon was an automaton that lit the fuse of the toy cannon, right?"

Abigail nodded.

"And the automaton, somehow, lit itself on fire. Maybe with a match. Maybe the same match that lit the cannon. That's my guess, anyway. It wouldn't be too hard to create an automaton that can light a match."

"Right," Grandma said. There was an impatient edge to her voice. Abigail didn't blame her; so far, none of the information was new or helpful.

"Well, the automaton burnt to ash, leaving only its metal parts behind, right?"

"Yes."

"A spring and a few screws."

Grandma shifted forward in her seat. "Yes, and?"

"Well, Shingo prides himself on only using springs and wood. I have this newspaper article from way back, ten years ago maybe. And in it, Shingo was being interviewed about what makes his devices so unique. Instead of using screws, glue, and what have you, Shingo makes his automata purely out of wood. He cuts the wood so precisely that all of the pieces fit together by themselves, no adhesion or screws needed. The *only* non-wood materials he uses are the springs."

Abigail concluded, "So, the automaton wasn't made by him. It was made by an impostor."

Guttler munched on a baby carrot. "Not a single piece in my extensive collection uses screws, I can tell you that much."

Abigail glanced at Grandma, who leaned forward. "You're unbanned from my store, Benjamin Guttler, but I'm still not selling you the squirrel nutcracker. Thank you for speaking with us."

Mr. Guttler took another bite out of the juicy chicken leg. "My pleasure. Hope it helps with the case. As for me, I'll return the cannon tonight, then I'm heading out of here tomorrow. Doesn't seem like anyone's going to part with their automata. They'll part with their giant tomatoes, sure, but not a single automaton. Where was that woman even growing tomatoes that size in winter?" He shook his head and chuckled. "The people in this town sure look out for one another."

"It's one of the many charms of living here," Grandma said, and the two women left Benjamin Guttler alone. Abigail threw the man one last look over her shoulder and was rather tickled to see the man as happy as a clam as he looked fondly over the rest of his dinner.

As they passed through the lobby, Abigail opened the front door and almost ran into a woman.

"Oh, excuse me," the woman muttered. She kept tugging at her red coat collar as if to hide her face, and she hardly spared a glance at Abigail as she hurried off toward the dining room.

"Wonder what's got her all wound up?" Abigail asked, holding the door open for Grandma. It wasn't until they were buckled in the car that it hit her.

"Grandma! I know that woman I almost ran into."

"Really? How?"

"She was at Shingo's grand reopening. I'm absolutely sure about it."

"And what about her left such an impression?"

"At first it was just that red coat. It's kinda hard to miss. But then I noticed she was acting weird. She kept looking around and she was definitely trying to hide something underneath her coat. Then, after the shot went off, I didn't see her again."

Grandma cranked up the heat and settled back in her seat. "That is peculiar. And, honestly, she reminded me of Shingo. Didn't she look as if she could be related to him?"

"Yeah, a little bit. Maybe we should ask Madeline if Shingo has any family members who might be holding a grudge against him."

"That's a great idea. But tonight, all I want is a hot shower and a soft Missy."

"I can't argue with that, Grandma." Abigail was also craving some hearty food, and she wondered what she could persuade Grandma to whip up for their evening. If they tried to question the flighty woman right now, she most certainly would skip town, so Abigail decided to let it go for the time being.

CHAPTER SEVENTEEN

Despite the following day being a Saturday when an influx of weekend tourists was to be expected, Grandma had declared the day off the night before.

As Abigail stretched in bed, nudging Thor with her elbow for extra space, she found herself feeling incredibly grateful that Grandma knew how to take some downtime. Abigail could take her time getting out of bed, go out for a leisurely run, and still make it home in time for a late morning coffee with Grandma.

So that's what Abigail did. When she felt good and ready, she rolled out of bed, bundled up in her running gear, and brushed her teeth and hair before heading downstairs. Thor followed happily at her heels and Missy was already waiting for her at the door.

They set out into the cold, quiet morning. All the

Christmas lights were still lit from the night before. Frost glazed over the long-browned grass, turning the neighborhood into a wintry ghost town. Even Camille wasn't poking around in her garden this morning.

After a long and satisfying run, the three made it back home. Missy and Thor flopped onto the floor in the kitchen to recover and wait for Grandma, but Abigail headed upstairs to shower, savoring the silence.

When she came back down, she had slipped back into her warm pajamas and her favorite fuzzy slippers; since the cold had started in earnest, the two Lane ladies had taken to having Saturday breakfast in their PJs.

Grandma was pouring coffee into two mugs as Abigail entered the kitchen and took a seat at the table. Grandma set the mugs down, along with a tiny glass pitcher of a thick, creamy liquid.

"What's that?" Abigail leaned toward the pitcher.

"It's sweetened condensed milk."

"For breakfast?"

"For your coffee. Have you ever tried it?"

"No."

"Well, stop fussing and pour a bit in there. My dear old friend Mrs. Applebaum showed me this trick. Don't add too much; it's quite rich and sweet."

"Who's Mrs. Applebaum again?"

"That's privileged information, dear. Now take a sip and tell me what you think."

Abigail took a sip of the steaming coffee. It was clearly a

dark roast, but the thick, sweet milk toned down the usual bitterness, leaving only a full, rich flavor.

"Wow, Grandma. That's delicious!"

"Why, thank you, dear. I find that it's nice to have every once in a while, especially when I'm feeling nostalgic over an old friend. Now, what would you like for breakfast?"

"Whatever your little granny heart desires."

"All right then." Grandma stood and moved to the refrigerator. "The works it is."

The older woman pulled out bacon, sausage, eggs, butter, and hash browns. Abigail loved watching her grandmother at work in the kitchen. She seemed so sure and confident when she prepared food, the way Camille always seemed so sure and confident about her plants. Abigail doubted that Grandma ever pulled open the refrigerator door just to gaze at its contents. She always knew what she wanted.

"Grandma, have you thought any more about Shingo's case?"

"Dear, I think I dream about the case these days. I have to admit, though, I'm pretty stumped."

"Me too." Abigail sighed. "Mr. Guttler is convinced Shingo didn't build the toy cannon or the automaton that triggered it. Even Madeline had said something about the screw being odd, now that I think about it. But if Shingo didn't build it, and Mr. Guttler has nothing to do with the murder, then who else could possibly be involved?"

"Maybe we're approaching this the wrong way."

"What do you mean?"

"Well, we keep starting from Shingo's end, trying to find proof that he didn't do it, or that someone else did."

"Yeah. Is there any other way to approach a murder case?"

"Sure there is. We focus on the victim."

"Dallas Redford?"

Grandma nodded. "We know now that he had some serious issues with Shingo years and years ago. Maybe we should try figuring out why he popped up again."

"But how?"

"Well, we've already talked to Madeline about Dallas, so I think that source is tapped out. The only other source of information I can think of is the paper."

"We both know how biased reporters can be in this town," Abigail said, thinking of the poor quality of the coverage surrounding the murder at Mary Chang's motel-now-hotel. "But, I'm not sure we have any other options."

"I've been keeping all the papers in a binder by my bed. Will you be a dear and run upstairs to fetch it?"

"Sure thing, Grandma." Abigail hustled up the stairs. Thor and Missy followed her, curious. When she dashed into Grandma's room and dashed right back out again a second later, the dogs were convinced she had invented a new game for them. They ran in and out of the room too, barking and bouncing, even after she headed back downstairs.

"Okay, I think I've got everything," she said, settling in at the table again. She opened the binder and began to carefully sort through the collected pages. After several minutes, she sighed and pushed the binder back. "All I can find is the same small article we read."

"Run the details by me again."

"Well, Dallas and Shingo were college roommates. The reporter did some digging and found that Shingo had submitted complaints about Dallas copying off his work and stealing his designs. Eventually, Dallas moved to a different room. Madeline also told us Dallas eventually moved away on his own, which isn't in this article. That's about all we've got."

"Hey, Grandma," Abigail began. "Let's try to get some information about that woman I ran into last night at the bed and breakfast. Think Madeline's up for some company?"

Grandma looked over at a container filled with her cookies. "Let's leave her with no choice. Not a person I know has ever turned down a batch of my cookies!"

Just then, someone knocked at the front door. The dogs, who were still playing in Grandma's room, thundered around on the floor over their heads before shooting down the stairs.

Abigail shot Grandma a questioning look. "Think it's a tourist?"

"If it is, they're about to be disappointed. Why don't you go look?"

Abigail padded out of the kitchen, through the store, and up to the front door. She peered through the curtain to see James on the porch, rubbing his hands together for warmth.

"It's James," Abigail called over her shoulder, totally aware he could hear her through the door. "Should I let him in?"

"Of course you should let him in. It's not his fault we're still in our pajamas."

Abigail tugged the door open and poked her head through the crack. "What do you want, detective?"

James laughed. "Still giving me a hard time, even after all the things we've been through. I just wanted to come inside and say hello to Granny Lane."

"Fine," Abigail said, nudging the door wider. "But we're not dressed for company."

"I'm not one for dressing up, so it makes no difference to me."

Abigail led the way to the kitchen. After James gave Grandma a big hug and a peck on the cheek, he settled down at the table next to Abigail. He noticed the newspaper binder and pulled it over to himself, flipping through its pages.

As he looked it over, he said, "Dad called me this morning sounding rather perplexed. It seems the cannon was returned last night, left by the back door at the station with a note taped to it that simply stated, 'Sorry.'" He continued thumbing through the pages, then glanced up at them when the room fell silent.

Abigail and Grandma shared a quick glance, then Grandma replied, "Isn't that strange, Abigail?"

Abigail answered with a smirk, "Indeed, Grandma."

James shook his head, "I'm not going to ask. I don't want to know."

Grandma replied, "That seems to be the best course of

action."

"Okay, so did you two come up with anything new?"

Grandma filled him in on their various conversations with Madeline and Benjamin Guttler, informing James that the potbellied collector was no longer a suspect on their list.

Abigail concluded, "What we're pretty positive about is that the automaton was not built by Shingo. Both Madeline and Mr. Guttler insist Shingo uses no metal except for springs in his creations."

"But if it wasn't Shingo, and if it wasn't Benjamin Guttler, then who was it?"

"That's what we're trying to figure out." Abigail slumped in her chair. "We were just looking into the victim when you showed up."

"Ah, Dallas Redford."

"That's our guy."

"Yeah, I did do a rudimentary online search of his name. It didn't yield much."

Abigail, kicking herself for not having consulted the internet sooner, whipped out her phone and conducted her own quick search. "Yeah, you're right. At least I'm not seeing anything that wasn't already in that newspaper article."

"Didn't make much of a name for himself, that's for sure."

Grandma brought two plates to the table and set them before Abigail and James.

"Oh, Granny Lane, you don't have to feed me. I didn't mean to barge in on your breakfast. Coffee is more than enough."

"Nonsense, we have plenty of food. And you're a growing boy."

James laughed. "About the only thing that's still growing is my hair." He shook his head, and his curls fell into his eyes.

"Hey, James," Abigail mused, picking up her fork. "Your dad's got access to police databases and whatnot. Has he found any helpful information there?"

"If he did, he hasn't told me. To be honest, even though he does deputize me now and again, he tries to leave me out of it otherwise."

"Why's that?" Grandma asked, taking a chair before her own plate of food, which may or may not have contained more than James's and Abigail's generous portions.

"I don't know. Guess he just never wanted the cop life for me. Not that he could stop me from starting my own PI business."

Grandma nodded slowly. "I can see why he wanted to keep you away from that life. It's very stressful, to say the least."

"It's all worked out in the end. I like being a free agent, so to speak." James's pocket buzzed, and he pulled out his phone to check the message. "Ah, speaking of, I'm working a local case right now and a lead just texted me some information."

Grandma took a big bite of her eggs before leaning forward. "Already doing PI work in town?"

"Yup. Fully licensed and everything."

"Sounds like you're planning on staying a while."

James winked at Grandma. "I just might. Abigail, maybe I

could pick your brain on this one? This case concerns you too, Granny, in a way."

"What's going on?" Grandma asked.

"Well, the recently named and now very official Granny Gang hired me to look into a secret crafter who's flooding the market with sock monkeys. It's lowering their bottom line, and we can't have that."

Abigail chuckled. "They hired you for *that?*"

"Don't make light of it, dear," Grandma said. Her expression seemed quite dire. "This sounds serious, and the culprit must be stopped. Why was I not told?" She arched an eyebrow at James.

James coughed. "Well, err, that's between you and the Gang. You've been busy lately with the recent murder and your shop, Granny. Anyhow, I was wondering if Abigail would like to come with me to help out in the case? That is, if you have the time. I could use the help."

Abigail wondered what his real motives were. The case sounded easy, but since he had helped her out before, she did owe him one. "Sure, I can help for a bit, but Grandma and I do have an errand to run later this morning."

Grandma waved Abigail off. "That's okay. It's too early to pop in on Madeline. And this new case seems quite dire. I mean, the nerve! I wonder if it's an out-of-towner?"

"I guess I'm joining you then, James. Let me get dressed, and I'll meet you outside."

"Great! Thanks, Cupcake." James stood and gave Grandma a hug. "Thank you for breakfast, Granny Lane."

CHAPTER EIGHTEEN

Abigail stepped outside and noticed it wasn't as cold as it was earlier. James headed straight for Grandma's pink golf cart, which was decorated with of all kinds of unnecessary bling. When she gave him a quizzical look, he said, "I thought we'd take this for a spin."

"Seriously? You're cool with being seen in that?"

"Sure. Why not? Besides, we need to be able to traverse the crowded streets. This is way better than my ride." He motioned toward his beat-up old sedan.

"I'm not gonna argue with you there." After unzipping the weather-resistant fabric panels, she climbed into the driver's seat of the golf cart and turned it on. She looked up at James and noticed he was digging through his trench coat's pockets instead of joining her. "Well, are you coming?"

"Just grabbing my monocular." He smiled and held up his

prized possession, a gift from her and Grandma. He then bent down and sat beside her, fixing the folds of his coat. A large errant curl plopped right between his eyes as he stared straight ahead with a huge smile on his face.

"Where to?" Abigail asked, suppressing the urge to brush his hair out of his eyes.

"Let's see if we can spot someone holding a knock-off monkey and simply ask where they got it."

"That's as good a plan as any." She pulled out and drove the cart as fast as it could handle—a measly fifteen miles an hour.

Soon, they found a spot downtown to park and exited the golf cart. The tourists were out in full swing, so James and Abigail easily blended into the crowd. Now they just had to find a sock monkey.

After a few minutes, Abigail spotted a young boy carrying what appeared to be a sock octopus. She tugged at James's left hand and pointed in the direction of the child and his parents. "Look at what that boy's carrying."

James looked through his monocular with his right hand, then lowered it. "Great eye, Cupcake."

Abigail quickly realized she was still holding James's hand and dropped it like it was on fire. "Okay. Now what?"

James chuckled. "I'll start with the parents." He cut through the crowd, Abigail following in his wake, until they reached their targets. He then tapped the father's shoulder. "Excuse me, sir."

The father and mother both turned. The small dark-haired boy clutched his mom's hand, the sock octopus firmly in his other arm.

"Yes? Can I help you?" the father asked.

James looked around sheepishly. "My girlfriend and I were hunting for a special Christmas gift for her nephew. And we couldn't help but notice that sock octopus your son's carrying. Do you mind telling me where you bought it?"

The father and mother both looked at each other, at the octopus, then back at James. The father began, "I'm sorry, we're not supposed to say—"

The mother pulled at the father's arm. "You're already saying too much!" She turned back to James. "Sorry, you'll have to get your nephew something else."

With that, the three of them hurried off.

"Well, that was strange," Abigail said, looking at the spot where they once stood.

"Did you see how quickly they took off? Like they were frightened to say anything more."

Abigail put a finger to her lip as she recalled the details. "Did you get a closer look at the sock octopus? Someone put a lot of effort into it, beyond anything I've seen from the Granny Gang's sock monkey collection. This craftsman is really something else. Whoever it is could put the Granny Gang out of business."

"Like I told them, there really is no law saying someone

else can't sell sock monkeys. The Granny Gang doesn't have a trademark on them or anything. Still, I offered my help in hopes that there could be a peaceful resolution. The last thing I want to see in Wallace Point is gang violence, especially of the geriatric variety."

"I agree. They take their turf very seriously."

"Well, let's check out the stores and see if any of them are selling the counterfeit monkeys. And keep your eye out for anyone else carrying."

After going through a couple of stores and talking with the owners, they passed Mr. Yamamoto's Toys and Games, seeing only a closed sign in the window. Abigail sighed despondently and looked at her watch. "We're going to have to wrap this up soon. We made plans to visit with Madeline this morning."

"This is certainly harder than I thought it would be. Let's swing by Sally's and see if she's heard anything."

"Sounds great. I could use some more caffeine."

THE MOMENT ABIGAIL and James entered the cafe, Sally spotted them and called out over her crowd of customers, "Hey you two! Grab a table. I'll bring you guys your usual in a few minutes and join you."

Abigail waved and joined James at a small bistro table he found in the corner. As she sat across from him, there was some kind of commotion at the entrance of the store. They both turned to see Sally's dad, Bobby, entering the store with all the usual ruckus the man was known for.

Bobby shot finger guns at his daughter, then made eye contact with Abigail and James, making a beeline right for them. "Good morning, you two!"

"Hey there, Bobby," James said as he stood and shook Bobby's hands, then returned to his seat. "Come join us."

Bobby pulled up a chair. "I can stay for a couple of minutes." He turned toward Abigail. "What new sleuthing are you up to today, Abigail?"

Abigail smiled. "Now, Bobby, who says I'm sleuthing?"

Bobby laughed a hard laugh that the situation didn't call for, but it was just his way. "You and James together? Must be sleuthing!" Then, he leaned in close, and whispered as best as he could accomplish for such a feat, which for most people was an ordinary volume. "That toy store murder—you must be knee-deep in it! I heard you were there!"

"Yeah, but I'm not sure I'm supposed to talk about it," Abigail whispered back, in a real whisper that Bobby didn't seem to hear.

"Yes, well, I'm sure it will all work out!" he said exuberantly. "It always does when you're on the case!"

James interrupted, "Bobby, you seem to have your finger on the pulse of this town. Any chance you've heard of a new sock monkey craftsman selling wares?"

Bobby frowned for a few moments. "No, I haven't. But I could ask this person to come forward on my next broadcast. It'll make for exciting television!"

"No, no. That's quite all right. We want to keep this on the down low, if you get my meaning."

"Oh, okay, James. My lips are sealed." Bobby looked like he was already about to explode with this new information, however. A rogue sock monkey maker was the type of hot gossip he could hardly keep to himself.

Right then, Sally appeared with a tray of drinks and snacks for the group. "Hey, Dad!" She placed the refreshments on the table and handed each person their special orders before leaning in to kiss her dad's cheek.

Bobby grabbed a scone off the tray, along with his drink, and stood up. "On that note, I'm off! Good luck on your hunt! I'll call if I spy anything of interest to you."

"Thank you, Bobby." Abigail waved as the man disappeared out the door. She then turned toward Sally, who took her dad's seat. "And thank you, Sally! I needed this." She sipped from her steaming cup of coffee.

"My pleasure." Sally turned to look at James. "You two look like you are up to something. Spill."

James coughed. "Are we that obvious?"

"Apparently we are," Abigail replied.

James shrugged like it couldn't be helped, then jumped right in. "Right. So, Sally, have you seen anyone with an unfamiliar style of sock monkey in the store?"

Sally laughed, almost spitting out some of her own coffee. "What an odd question. Are you two on some kind of sock monkey caper?"

"As it so happens, yes," James replied simply, looking a

little embarrassed.

Abigail intervened, "It would seem someone has infiltrated our town, selling bootleg sock monkeys without the express consent of the Granny Gang."

"Oh no!" Sally responded, mostly in jest. "We can't have that!"

James stated, "It does seem rather silly at the moment, with a murder investigation going on. But since my father doesn't want to involve me with that case, I thought the least I could do was help the Granny Gang."

Abigail added, "Since so many people pass through here every day, we were wondering if you'd mind keeping an eye out for anyone carrying impostor sock monkeys, and if you see any, see if you can get them to tell you who their dealer is."

"Of course, of course. I'd be delighted to help out. James, are they paying you for this endeavor? I'm sure you have better things to do or bigger fish to fry."

James laughed. "Actually, I just wrapped up a case that paid rather handsomely, so I accepted this case pro bono." He leaned in closer and whispered, "Although they *did* insist they would make it worth my while."

Abigail grinned. "Oh no. That sounds a little sinister, knowing them. It could mean anything."

James suddenly looked worried and asked, "Really? I was thinking they meant a casserole or baked goods or something."

Abigail patted his shoulder. "It's probably something

innocent." She then winked at Sally.

"I saw that wink!" James teased.

Sally looked off, a frown beginning to form across her brow. Both Abigail and James grew quiet as they watched her, wondering if she was remembering a critical clue.

All of a sudden, she jumped up. "I'm sorry, but I gotta get back to the kitchen! I just remembered I've got scones in the oven. I'll talk to you two later, okay?" Without waiting for a response, she zipped through the crowded tables and disappeared into the back of the store.

"I wonder what that was about?" Abigail asked.

"No idea," James responded. "You would think she'd have a timer on if she were baking something."

Abigail was just about to pursue that line of thinking when she looked at her watch. "Oh, dang. I have to run."

"I understand. Don't let me keep you."

"I'm sorry we didn't get anywhere."

"No, we did good. Few cases are solved in a day, especially one as harrowing as this. We put a couple of feelers out there so something will turn up soon. Let's head back."

Abigail stood up and followed him out the door, pausing to wave to Sally before leaving.

Sally was helping a customer, but paused to wave back. Her smile looked slightly devious, which left Abigail wondering if this sock monkey case went deeper than they thought.

The town of Wallace Point was always up to something, that was for sure.

CHAPTER NINETEEN

Once Abigail got back home, she and Grandma headed straight to the Yamamoto house. They hadn't called beforehand, so when Grandma knocked on the door, she brandished her container of cookies like a sugar shield. They heard steps approach and pause at the peephole, so Abigail and Grandma threw on their most winning smiles for whoever was peering at them.

After a moment, the door opened and Madeline's face emerged, her expression unreadable. "Good morning."

Grandma smiled. "Good morning, Madeline. I apologize for coming over unannounced. We brought you some more cookies. We were hoping to pick your brain about some ideas we have for the case."

Madeline searched Grandma's face before allowing her gaze to linger on the container in the older woman's hands.

Finally, Madeline stepped aside. "Please, come in. Hanako isn't here just now. She's at a friend's house."

Madeline led the way to the kitchen, which looked radically different from their previous visit. Nearly every square inch of available counter space was piled high with mountains of baked goods.

"My!" Grandma gushed. "You sure have a lot of food here."

A soft smile played around Madeline's lips. "You know, it's the strangest thing. Remember the night you visited? Up until then, I hadn't received a single casserole or baked good from any of my neighbors. But that very evening people started popping up on my doorstep. They haven't stopped since."

"Well, that's nice, dear. Your neighbors must really love you."

"I hardly know what to do with all the food," Madeline said, glancing at her crowded, cluttered kitchen, so different from the rest of her home. "But I am grateful for their kind thoughts. I was really starting to feel the whole town was against Shingo."

Abigail eased into a chair at the table and opened the container of cookies. "Would you like to know what we've learned so far?"

Madeline grabbed three plates and a pile of napkins before settling in beside Abigail. "Yes, please."

Abigail told her the same information she'd shared with

James. She was honest and direct, which Madeline seemed to appreciate.

"So, you've ruled out that collector, and you're stuck when it comes to Dallas Redford," Madeline summarized.

"Yes, but we do have another suspect. That's actually why we wanted to speak with you. On the night of the reopening, I noticed a woman who was acting pretty strange. She kept sneaking looks around and she was definitely trying to hide something under her coat. But I lost track of her when Shingo opened the doors. I didn't see her again the rest of that evening."

Madeline nodded, attentive yet silent.

"Last night, I ran into her again at the bed and breakfast downtown. She seemed just as stressed as she was that night at the reopening. I don't think she recognized me, but I sure recognized her. Grandma saw her too, and pointed out to me that she looked remarkably like Shingo. Do you know of any woman related to Shingo who might have had a problem with him?"

Madeline's face wore a thoughtful expression. "As a matter of fact, I might know someone who fits that description. Would you wait here for just a minute?"

"Of course," Grandma said kindly.

Madeline disappeared into the living room, and Abigail and Grandma shot eager looks at each other. When the woman returned, she had an old photo album under her arm. She set it on the table, flipped the book open, and gently extricated an old photo. She set the picture in front of Abigail and Grandma.

Abigail's heart leaped into her throat as she studied the photo. It showed a much younger Shingo. He was still a teen —and an early teen at that. He sat on a bench in a park. Beside him sat a girl about the same age, grinning just as widely as he was. The girl's face was relaxed and happy. She strongly resembled Shingo and only loosely resembled the anxious woman Abigail kept seeing. But there wasn't a doubt in Abigail's mind that the two were the same person.

"What do you think, Abigail?" Grandma asked.

"Yeah. That's her. Who is she?"

"Yuri, a cousin of Shingo's. I never met her myself, but I know they were pretty close, like a brother and sister. Then they had some sort of falling out."

"What happened?"

"I don't know. Shingo never really told me. I always thought they'd simply grown out of their childhood friend-ship. But I guess something more could have happened between them."

"Yuri was holding onto something, keeping it tucked away in her coat," Abigail mused. "It was small, whatever it was. Maybe the size of one of Shingo's automata…"

Grandma's eyebrows arched. "Now *that* could be an important detail, don't you think?"

"I'm starting to think it is, yeah."

"Maybe she's the one who set up the trap automaton?"

"She was acting pretty shifty for sure. Did she talk to Shingo at all?"

Madeline shook her head. "I was with him almost the entire time. I'm sure I would have noticed his reaction to seeing her after all of these years."

"So Yuri kept away from him, using the crowd to go unnoticed... and once the shot went off, I didn't see her again. Not until I ran into her at the bed and breakfast."

"But why would she still be here?" Grandma asked.

"Well," Abigail began slowly. "I get the feeling that if Yuri was the one who planted the trap automaton, then she didn't mean for it to kill Dallas. She and Dallas have no connection, or if they did, it'd be a huge coincidence and wouldn't make much sense."

Madeline nodded. "Her friendship with Shingo ended long before he met Dallas. This picture of them might be the last one they ever took together."

"Which could mean that the automaton wasn't ever meant for Dallas. It was meant for Shingo."

Grandma leaned forward. "What do you think her motive was?"

Abigail added, "What could she achieve by killing Shingo? What would she get out of it?"

Grandma suggested, "Satisfaction? The end of a years' long dispute?"

Madeline glanced between the two women before getting up from the table. She collected the used plates and carried them to the sink. Her manner was calm, but a mask had slipped over her face, cool and impenetrable.

Abigail noticed and immediately felt awful. She was pretty sure Madeline only put that mask on when she needed to keep herself together. "Sorry, Madeline. Grandma and I can get kinda carried away sometimes."

Madeline shook her head. "I really hope you're wrong about Yuri. The thought of her trying to kill Shingo over some childhood dispute…" She broke off, and pressed her lips into a hard line.

Grandma stood and moved toward Madeline. She put a hand on her arm and said softly, reassuringly, "Don't worry, Madeline. We're going to get to the bottom of it. We always do."

Madeline took a deep breath. She released it gently and looked into Grandma's eyes. "Thank you, Florence."

After that, Grandma and Abigail didn't linger at the Yamamoto house. Despite the casseroles and baked goods, Madeline was clearly suffering; at least, it was clear to Grandma and Abigail now that they knew her a bit better.

Once they were back in the car, Abigail turned to Grandma. "So, Yuri is suspect number one now, right?"

"Sadly, I think she is. I hate squabbles between family members. It's such a shame."

"Well, we already know where she's staying. Why don't we go see what we can learn from her?"

Grandma nodded. "Lead the way, dear." As Abigail started

the car, Grandma had a smirk on her face that she was clearly trying to suppress.

"What are you smirking about?"

"Just how chock-full of comfort food her counter was," Grandma said smugly. "You can always count on the Granny Gang to pull through."

CHAPTER TWENTY

The drive to the bed and breakfast was a short one, but it took them twice as long as usual to reach it.

"Tourists," Grandma groaned for the umpteenth time.

They were everywhere. They crowded the sidewalks, spilled onto the streets, and ignored crossing lanes and lights. Sally's Book Cafe was full to overflowing, making Abigail smile. Sally certainly deserved the business.

Finally, Abigail's Bug crawled into the parking lot of the bed and breakfast. With relieved sighs, the Lanes climbed out of the car and stretched their limbs.

"Dodging tourists is almost as stressful as Boston traffic," Abigail said. "I was looking out for Yuri the whole drive but didn't see her."

"She must be hiding out at the bed and breakfast. Should we try to confront her?"

Abigail shook her head. "Let's play it by ear. We have nothing but circumstantial evidence against her. And I'm not even sure it can be called evidence yet. I want to try to meet her in a sort of casual fashion, you know? Not let her know we're suspicious of her."

"Yes, that's probably the best way to go about it."

They walked into the building and looked around. Yuri wasn't in the lobby, or in the living room with the fireplace, or in the nearly empty dining room. But Benjamin Guttler was sitting at the same table as the night before. If it hadn't been for his change of clothing, Abigail would have wondered whether the man had ever left his seat.

Abigail glanced at Grandma, who responded with a short nod. They slipped into the dining room and into the chairs next to Mr. Guttler.

"Good morning, ladies," Mr. Guttler said around a mouthful of bagel. "I sure hope you're not here to interrogate me further. I told you everything I know."

"Of course not," Grandma cooed. Her tone was much more agreeable than the night before, and her face shone with the forced enthusiasm of a shop assistant. Abigail had to suppress a giggle, but Mr. Guttler didn't seem to notice. "How's breakfast?"

"Excellent, just excellent. I must say, for such a small town, Wallace Point sure has some decent cooks."

"So, Mr. Guttler," Abigail said. "Have you seen a woman with long black hair around here? She often wears a red coat."

Mr. Guttler continued to chomp on his bagel, but his forehead creased in concentration. "Oh, actually, I think I have."

When he didn't elaborate further, Abigail pressed, "And what can you tell us about her?"

"Hmm. Well, after the murder happened, I had worked up quite the appetite, so I had an extended dinner here. I noticed the woman you described at one of the tables. She looked rather upset, and she hardly touched her plate. I remember thinking it was a terrible shame for her home-made chicken pot pie to go to waste." Mr. Guttler shook his head, and his eyes took on a sad, faraway look. "A terrible shame."

Abigail blinked. Did this guy only think with his stomach? "So," she pressed. "Did you talk to her?"

Mr. Guttler finished his bagel and started on his bowl of cheesy grits. "Of course. I asked her if she was going to finish the pot pie, and she kindly let me have it. She seemed upset, so I took a seat at her table and asked what was wrong. She mentioned the shooting at the store, said it really had her shook up."

"Did she say anything about Shingo?"

Finally, Mr. Guttler seemed to pick up on how interested Grandma and Abigail seemed to be in the woman with the long black hair. He narrowed his eyes. "Now, you two aren't going to go harass that poor woman like you did me, are you?"

"Harass?" Grandma laughed. "We didn't harass you, Mr.

Guttler. Really, you harassed us. In fact, you've harassed several members of the Wallace Point community. A little bird even told me Piper Fischer aimed a musket at you."

Mr. Guttler had the decency to blush. He took several deep swallows of chocolate milk and waved a hand dismissively. "Misunderstandings, all of them. Now, what were you asking?"

"Did the woman say anything about Shingo?"

"Oh, you know, now that I think about it... I had asked her if she was a fan of Shingo's. I thought that was a safe, pleasant question, since she had traveled here for the reopening. But she avoided the question and then invented some excuse to head up to her room."

"How do you know she made the excuse up?"

"I may be tenacious," Mr. Guttler chuckled, pausing from his eating, "but I'm not oblivious to social cues. I can tell when someone doesn't want to hang around me. It's just that I usually don't care!" He gave a cheeky smile.

Grandma glanced at Abigail before putting a gentle hand to Mr. Guttler's elbow. "Have you seen her lately?"

"Sure, sure. Only an hour ago I caught a glimpse of her hurrying out the front entrance. It looked like she headed left down the street, but I can't be too sure."

"Thank you, Mr. Guttler," Grandma said with more sincerity in her voice than at the start of the conversation. "We'll leave you to your breakfast, now. You've been wonderfully patient. If you ever return to Wallace Point, stop by the store. I won't sell my nutcracker to you, but you're welcome to a cookie."

Benjamin Guttler wiped his mouth and grinned broadly. Once again, Abigail was reminded of his strong resemblance to snowmen. All he needed was a pipe. "That's very kind of you, Florence. It will be nice to have a friend in this feisty little town."

Grandma and Abigail headed back outside, turning left at the street. They were in the thick of downtown—and of the tourists. The crush of people was so intense that the Lane ladies almost lost each other. Finally, Grandma linked her arm through Abigail's and cleared a path for the two of them with a determined glare, which the tourists dared not confront.

They ducked into every shop they came across. Each shop was crowded, loud, and too warm after the freshness of the cold outdoors. They didn't linger, and soon they came to Kirby's Candlepin Bowling Alley with its humble little wreath on the front door. They stepped inside, waited in a corner while their eyes adjusted to the relative dimness, and saw Yuri sitting at the bar.

"There she is," Abigail whispered, as if Grandma wasn't seeing the same thing she was. "Should we talk to her?"

"Definitely."

They took one more moment to observe her from afar. She was nursing a half-empty glass of beer. Abigail commented, "Doesn't it seem a bit early to be drinking?"

Grandma shrugged. "I'm not going to complain. People tend to be more talkative after a few drinks."

Abigail couldn't argue with that, so she walked to the bar and took a seat next to Yuri. The woman glanced at her before looking away again, and Abigail was struck by how much she resembled Shingo. How had she not seen it before?

Grandma slid into the seat next to Abigail, flicking her eyebrows at Yuri. Abigail understood what she was trying to communicate; after all, anyone with eyes could see Yuri was drinking to forget, not drinking for fun. If her dejected demeanor wasn't enough to give it away, her wet eyes certainly were.

Kirby came up to them to take their orders. He kept as much distance between himself and Yuri as he possibly could, and he looked at Abigail with a certain amount of desperation in his eyes. Abigail had to stifle a giggle. Was big, stern Kirby afraid of a crying woman?

"Coffee for us both, please, Kirby," she said, then glanced sideways at Yuri. "And another beer for her."

Kirby walked off to make the coffee. Yuri sniffled, cast another look at Abigail, then returned her gaze to her nearly empty glass. "Thanks, I guess, but I was just about to go."

"Where to?" Abigail asked.

Yuri hesitated before answering simply, "My room."

"Ah. What brings you to Wallace Point?"

Yuri sighed and drained the last of her beer. "I don't know. A dumb little whim."

Grandma got up from her seat next to Abigail and slipped

into the empty seat on Yuri's other side. Yuri stiffened, but she didn't look at Grandma. For a minute, no one said anything. Yuri shifted in her seat and mumbled, "I think I'm going to go."

"It's a shame what happened to Shingo, isn't it?" Grandma began. "Such a talented man, with such a beautiful family."

Kirby came up just then. He set a beer in front of Yuri and coffees in front of Grandma and Abigail before backing away slowly, as if Yuri was a ticking time bomb of tears.

Yuri took a long drink from her glass. When she set it down, she squinted up at Grandma and Abigail in turn. "Yeah, sure, it'd be a shame... if he wasn't apparently the murderer."

"Who says he is?" Grandma asked in her kindest old lady voice. "He hasn't been convicted."

Grandma's act seemed to work. Yuri relaxed and took another sip. "Maybe. I don't know. That's just what the papers say."

"And what exactly do they say?" Abigail asked. "I haven't had the chance to read up on what happened." Of course, just a few short hours before, she had studied all of the articles again. If Yuri mentioned any details that hadn't actually been reported, Abigail was sure she'd catch them.

Yuri looked at her incredulously. Abigail figured she was wondering why two locals were asking a tourist about the town's news. "Well, they say that the murder victim was an old peer of his. And they say the murder weapon was some kind of toy, like the ones he makes. That's all I know."

"Do you know Shingo personally?" Grandma used the same quivering, disarming tone and looked into Yuri's dark eyes gently.

For a moment, Yuri looked taken aback by the question, and Abigail was sure she would bolt. Instead, she seemed to melt under Grandma's warm gaze.

"I used to," she said at last, her voice weak. "I guess I don't anymore. Thanks for the drink." She stood, threw her coat over her shoulders, and trudged out the door.

Kirby crept up as soon as she was gone. "New suspect?"

Abigail shook her head. "I'm not sure. Did she say anything to you before we got here?"

"She's quiet, like me. And she was crying. So I left her alone."

"Shame on you, Kirby," Grandma teased. "A handsome strapping man like you letting that poor soul cry by herself."

Kirby, usually so dire that he sometimes scared away tourists, blushed with embarrassment and shame. "Granny Lane, I... err... she—"

Grandma burst out laughing. "Kirby, never change. I love you just the way you are."

Rather than looking relieved, Kirby blushed even more deeply. Abigail couldn't help but join in Grandma's laughter, and soon, Kirby just grabbed a rag and moved away to buff an already gleaming table.

Abigail made sure to tip Kirby extra before they, too, headed out. "I wish Kirby was more of a gossip."

"Still," Grandma said thoughtfully. "Yuri didn't say anything that contradicted what was in the paper."

"She seemed more than happy to call him guilty, though."

"Happy? I don't know. She didn't seem very happy to me."

Abigail's shoulders slumped. "That conversation wasn't quite the smoking gun I was hoping it'd be."

"We'll figure it out." Grandma patted Abigail's shoulder.

They climbed into the car to head for home. After the excitement of the morning, Abigail was more than ready to curl up in front of the fire with Thor and a good book. Still, she felt frustrated. They had ruled out Benjamin Guttler as a suspect, and now Grandma no longer seemed as convinced about Yuri's involvement.

But if the murderer wasn't Mr. Guttler or Yuri, then who could it be? Who framed Shingo, and why? Or was the case really as simple as it seemed, and Shingo really did do it?

Abigail couldn't bear the thought.

CHAPTER TWENTY-ONE

Abigail and Grandma spent the rest of the weekend holed up inside the house. They ventured out in the evenings to walk around the neighborhood and admire all the Christmas cheer. For the most part, though, they cuddled in front of the fire with the dogs, drank hot cocoa and tea, and ate all of the homiest foods Grandma could think of.

When Monday morning rolled around, the Lane women felt rested and well-prepared to face another week of Christmas tourists. The morning passed quickly from sheer busyness until they hit a lull just before lunch, and Grandma decided to lock up a couple of minutes early.

"Hey, Grandma," Abigail called as she finished reconciling the cash register. "You pick up on any gossip today?"

"Nothing useful. I've been thinking about calling Willy,

but he seems to be deliberately keeping us out of this case. Normally, he tells me much more about what's going on."

"You don't think he actually suspects Shingo, do you?"

"To be honest, dear, I haven't the faintest idea. At first, I thought he was giving me space so I wouldn't chew his head off. That was wise on his part, of course. But then I got to thinking about what James told us. He said Willy made him promise not to get us involved. If I had to guess, Willy is just trying to protect us ladyfolk. He can be a bit old fashioned like that."

"We don't have time for old fashioned," Abigail grumbled. "Christmas is just around the corner."

Grandma nodded, and her lips jutted out in a pout. Despite her annoyance with Sheriff Wilson, Abigail couldn't help but smile as she watched her grandmother. The small woman was just so adorable. Christmas really was around the corner, and it would be the first one she had ever shared with Florence Lane.

For so many years, Abigail had thought the only family member she had left was her mother, who wasn't the Christmas type. Or the holiday type. Or the birthday type.

Now that she'd found Grandma, though, Abigail's heart was full in a way it hadn't been before. Instead of feeling lonely, she felt loved and needed. It was a wonderful way to feel for the holidays, and it made her realize three things.

The first was that she wanted to make this Christmas special. Abigail had no idea how she was going to make that happen, but she was determined to figure something out.

The second thing she realized was that she never wanted to feel lonely on Christmas again, and the third thing was she didn't want anyone else feeling lonely either—Shingo and his family included.

"Hey," Grandma said slowly, interrupting Abigail's thoughts. "I think I have an idea."

"Let's hear it."

"Well, I know Willy gets coffee a couple of times a day at Sally's Book Cafe. I just don't know the exact times he goes."

Abigail nodded. "I'm on it."

She pulled her phone from her back pocket and typed a quick message to Sally. Abigail put her phone down, expecting Sally to take a while to respond. Not even a minute later, the phone beeped with a new message alert. Abigail read the text and grinned.

"She expects he'll come in during the lunch hour."

"Then we'll lie in wait," Grandma said, her eyes narrowing and an impish smile spreading across her face. "It's a good thing we closed early. Let's take the golf cart. Easier to hide."

Fifteen minutes later, they pulled into a parking spot across the street from Sally's. Tourists streamed along the sidewalks and roads, their cheeks and noses red from the cold.

"Did we miss him?" Abigail asked. She tried to peer

through the big glass windows of the Book Cafe, but there were too many people lined up outside for her to get a clear view.

"I don't see his car. Oh, wait! Abigail, there it is!" Grandma pointed at a patrol car as it coasted up the street and pulled into a parallel parking spot right in front of the cafe. Sure enough, Sheriff Wilson climbed out. They saw him survey the line, then shrug his shoulders and take his place at the very end.

"Looks like we have a minute before he actually makes it inside."

"Let's wait out here," Grandma suggested. "If he sees us before he makes it inside, he might just jump back in his car and forgo the coffee. Besides, sitting in this cart beats standing in that line."

So they waited. The line really was long, but Sally must have been working hard because people moved forward faster than Abigail would have expected. After just a few minutes, Sheriff Wilson slipped into the cafe.

Grandma and Abigail climbed out of the golf cart, being careful to zip up the fabric cover behind them. When they made it inside, Sheriff Wilson was at the counter, giving his order to Sally. She caught sight of them and flashed a quick bright smile before turning to get to work on Sheriff Wilson's coffee. Sheriff Wilson followed the direction of her gaze and saw Grandma and Abigail making a beeline for him.

The man looked spooked. His body went rigid, and his

eyes danced around looking for an escape path. But by then it was too late. They were on him in moments, and even over the general din in the cafe Abigail heard the Sheriff moan. She almost felt bad for him. Almost.

"All right," he sighed. "Just ask me whatever it is you're going to ask."

Grandma frowned. "Don't be like that, Willy. You know I only want to help."

"Sure, Florence."

His words surprised Abigail. Usually the man doted on her grandmother, but today he seemed tired, defeated.

"Did you know Shingo never puts metal screws in his automata?" Grandma asked. Her voice was even and brisk, and she kept a careful eye on Sheriff Wilson's face.

"Yes, yes. We've already explored that line of investigation. It's not enough to exonerate him."

Abigail cast a quick look at Sally. The girl was moving slowly, and she kept looking over her shoulder at them. She winked at Abigail when she caught her gaze.

Grandma's frown deepened. "If you need more proof, I'm willing to let you look over every automaton I have that he's made. I even have some that date back to when he was a teenager. I'm telling you: you won't find any screws."

"I appreciate that, Florence, but he's already confessed in great detail."

Abigail's stomach dropped. Grandma didn't seem like she was handling the news too well either. She swayed slightly, and Sheriff Wilson gently took her elbow to steady her.

"What do you mean, Willy?"

"I didn't believe it either, Florence. Not at first." Sheriff Wilson paused to clear his throat. When he continued, his voice was gruff. "But he drew up the schematics to the trap automaton to prove he made it. The springs and screws match up perfectly to the evidence. I didn't let him so much as take a glance into the room after the cannon went off, so there's no way he could have seen the remaining metal pieces and reverse-engineered the device."

Tears pooled in Grandma's eyes, and Abigail felt her brain cloud. Shingo had confessed. Not only that, but he'd proven his own guilt. She didn't know what to think. She'd known, she'd been absolutely sure, that Shingo was not guilty. Could she have been wrong?

"Wait," Abigail said, a sudden thought surfacing in the fog that enveloped her brain. "What about the fact that the door was locked from the inside?"

Sheriff Wilson shrugged. "I'm still trying to piece that all together myself. But as far as what we *do* know, he's not looking very innocent. Heck, when he first showed me the schematics, I suggested he get a lawyer for his own sake. He refused."

Sheriff Wilson studied them both, then turned to Sally, who was still working away at his drink. "It's safe to wrap it up now, Sally. I think these ladies got all the information they came for."

Blushing, Sally slid a cardboard cozy over the to-go cup

and handed the coffee to Sheriff Wilson. "Sorry about the delay, Sheriff."

Sheriff Wilson didn't comment. He simply handed her his money and turned back to Abigail and Grandma. "I'm thinking this is one you two can't solve. I'm sorry to say it, I really am, but it's not looking good for Shingo."

The sheriff reached out and touched Grandma's elbow one more time before making his way out of the crowded cafe.

Sally cleared her throat. "Well, that sounds like a direct challenge, doesn't it?"

"It does," Grandma murmured. Then, she lifted her chin and met Sally's eyes. "Willy should know I don't give up that easily."

Sally set two to-go cups on the counter. "Here, some caffeine for you two on the house. I made them when I should have been making Willy's. I get the feeling you're gonna need this."

CHAPTER TWENTY-TWO

B ack in the golf cart, Abigail and Grandma sat for a silent minute, watching the red-nosed tourists bustle along the sidewalks.

"Do you think he actually did it, Grandma?"

"Not for one second."

"Then why would he confess?"

"That's what we've got to find out. He apparently feels some kind of responsibility in all of this. We know he didn't murder anyone. What else could he have done that would make him feel guilty?"

Abigail shook her head. "I have no idea. It just doesn't make any sense. How was that room still locked? And why was it locked to begin with?"

Grandma turned the key and started the golf cart. "I think we need to pay Madeline another visit."

"Now? I can't imagine she's doing too well."

"That's exactly why we should see her. We need answers, and I'm thinking she could use a shoulder to lean on."

BY NOW, the drive to the Yamamoto house was a familiar one, but Abigail felt like it grew more daunting each time they made it. The secluded street felt lonelier, the woods thicker and taller. Abigail caught herself shivering from more than just the cold.

Empty-handed this time, Abigail and Grandma marched up to the door and knocked. It was a while before the door swung open, and it was Hanako who looked up at them rather than Madeline.

"Granny Lane!" Hanako threw herself into Grandma's arms. "Did you bring more cookies?"

"Not this time, dear. Is your mother home?"

"Yes. She asked me to welcome you in. She knew it'd be you two." Hanako took Grandma's hand and led the Lane women to the dining room.

Abigail noted that the house looked entirely the same, but there was a new stillness, a profound silence she hadn't felt before. She wondered if Hanako felt it too.

"Please, wait here," Hanako said politely. "Mama is in her room, but she'll be right down. I'll get the tea started."

"Do you need help with the stove, dear?"

Hanako blinked at Grandma. "No, thank you, Granny Lane."

The small girl scampered to the kitchen and tugged a folding stepladder out from behind the refrigerator. She unfolded it, grabbed the waiting teapot from the stove, then nudged the stool over to the sink. She climbed up, filled the pot with water, then pulled the stool back over to the stove, setting the teapot carefully on an eye. When she was satisfied, she folded the step-ladder and placed it back behind the fridge.

She made her way back to Grandma's side. "Mama should be down any second. Is there anything else I can get for you while you're waiting?"

"No, Hanako, you've done plenty. But don't you want to wait here with us?"

Hanako shook her head. "I'm working on Papa's Christmas gift. I've got a lot to do before I'm done." The little girl glanced over her shoulder, then said in a quieter voice, "Do you know when he's coming home?"

Abigail tensed, but she was careful to keep her face neutral. Grandma managed to do the same.

"I'm sorry, honey, I'm afraid I don't know."

Hanako's slim shoulders slumped. "Okay. Thanks, Granny Lane. I just wish I knew how much time I had to finish this thing." She turned and scurried silently back up the stairs.

Grandma took a deep breath, and Abigail did the same.

They waited in the quiet Yamamoto house for a moment before hearing light footsteps patter down the stairs.

Madeline's hair was wet, and she had combed and plaited it so that it hung in a glossy rope down her back. Without a word, she walked up to Grandma and hugged her.

Grandma wrapped her arms around Madeline and held the woman tight as quiet sobs shook her slight frame. Abigail closed her eyes, trying to choke back the lump rising in her throat.

The kettle began to sing. Abigail opened her eyes and saw Madeline draw in a shuddering breath before pulling gently away from Grandma. She moved to the stove and pulled the kettle off the heat.

"You heard the news, then," she said.

"We inquired. I don't think Shingo's confession is common knowledge."

Abigail saw Madeline's back stiffen. The kettle shook in her hand and she set it gently back onto the kitchen counter.

"How am I supposed to tell Hanako? It wouldn't be right to keep the truth from her, but at the same time, if I tell her, she'll be completely devastated."

"It's not the truth yet," Grandma insisted. "But if there's any chance that he's innocent, we'll need all the information we can get to put the pieces together. If you want us to dig deeper into this, you'll need to tell us everything."

Madeline turned to face Grandma. The smooth, controlled mask she usually wore was nowhere to be seen.

Her eyes were red, and there were new lines etched into her forehead.

"What do you need to know?"

"For one, why does Shingo keep that room locked? Such a secure room is a suspiciously prime place to cook up a murderous automaton."

"That's for Hanako's protection," Madeline explained. "It was my idea." Her chin trembled and she turned back around to place a hand on the kettle again. "He keeps his power tools in there, and since Hanako can be just a little too curious sometimes, we both decided to keep that room locked up for her safety."

A thought crossed Abigail's mind. "What more can you tell us about Dallas Redford?"

"Not much honestly," Madeline said, but then she hesitated.

"What is it, Madeline?"

"Well, I can tell you that I don't mind that he's dead."

Considering the history and circumstances, Abigail wasn't at all shocked by Madeline's admission. Yet something told her to keep digging. "Why not?"

"He was a real creep, back when I knew him in college."

"You knew him personally?"

"Not really, but that didn't keep him from somehow taking every class I took. This was after he and Shingo had their initial falling out, when Shingo got him moved to another room. Shingo was acting really distant during that semester, so he and I drifted apart for a short while."

"Because he was stressed out about Dallas stealing his work and breaking into his room?"

"Yes. I think at one point Dallas was even rummaging around in Shingo's trash. I didn't know that at first, though. I thought Shingo just didn't like me anymore. So, Dallas tried swooping in while I was unaware of what had happened between them."

"What then?" Grandma asked.

"We sorta talked at first. Dallas was kinda funny and charming. But eventually, Shingo told me what happened, and I realized that Dallas was just putting on an act. Maybe he thought he could get at Shingo by dating me or something."

"This Dallas fellow sounds like he used to be quite the petty type."

"He was." Madeline nodded, her eyes on Grandma.

"If either of them were to commit murder, my money would have been on Dallas, not Shingo."

Madeline looked away. "Yeah, but Shingo confessed."

Though she could only see Madeline's profile, Abigail saw a tear roll down her cheek. The more Abigail heard about Dallas, the less she liked the guy. But while the fact that he hit on Madeline to get back at Shingo was both creepy and downright mean, it didn't really add up to anything helpful.

She still thought the cheap workmanship of the trap automaton was proof enough that Shingo didn't make it. And if he didn't make it, then he obviously couldn't have killed Dallas. She opened her mouth to prod further, then snapped it shut.

Hanako's footsteps rumbled down the stairs. Madeline turned quickly to the sink to splash her face with cold water. When Hanako ran into the living room, her mother turned and smiled brightly.

"Hanako, you did a wonderful job of greeting our guests. Thank you very much for your help."

Hanako smiled, but there was a shadow of doubt in her eyes. The cold water hadn't been enough to clear all traces of sorrow from Madeline's face. Hanako glanced at Grandma, then back at her mother.

"Mom, can we have lunch soon?"

"Of course. I was just about to get started on it." Madeline turned to Granny and Abigail, her smile tight. "Would you two join us?"

"Oh, no," Grandma said. "We've got to get back to the store. Antiques don't sell themselves, you know. But thank you for the invitation. And Hanako, thank you for your hospitality."

Hanako nodded, then turned to her mother. "Do you mind if I keep working on Papa's gift until lunch is ready?"

"That's fine, but I expect you to help me with dinner."

"Yes, Mama." Hanako hugged Grandma, shot Abigail a friendly smile, then ran back up the stairs.

"She seems to be in a fairly good mood." Grandma smiled.

"When they first took Shingo away, I had told her that it

was a mistake, and that he'd be back home before she knew it. She doesn't know anything else yet."

Grandma stood, walked over to Madeline, and took her hand. "You wait before telling her anything, okay? Not until it's final."

Madeline hesitated, her eyes flitting up to the ceiling, where Hanako's footsteps could occasionally be heard. "Okay. I'll wait."

Grandma squeezed her hand one more time before she and Abigail made their way to the front door.

CHAPTER TWENTY-THREE

Abigail found it surprisingly easy to paste a fake smile on her face for all the customers loitering about the antique store.

"Sorry we're late," she announced cheerfully.

"Come right on in," Grandma cooed.

They were half an hour late in opening after lunch, and some of the tourists weren't happy about it. One or two of them had that aggrieved, smug look in their eyes that promised a heck of a time haggling. Abigail decided to slip into the kitchen. Her stomach rumbled, and she figured Grandma was just as hungry as she was.

She poked around in the pantry until she found sliced bread. From the fridge she pulled a jar of strawberry preserves. She took her time spreading peanut butter on the soft white slices, thankful for a minute to wrap her head around everything she'd learned over lunch.

Shingo had confessed to the murder. He'd even provided proof of his guilt. Madeline apparently believed her husband's confession and was steeling herself to break the news to Hanako.

Abigail forced the girl's face out of her mind and focused, instead, on all of the inconsistencies. Why had the door been locked from the inside? Why would Dallas Redford reappear now, after years of silence? Why would Shingo kill the washed-up man who could no longer pose any real threat to his work and relationships?

She shook her head. Deep down, she still believed that Shingo was innocent. But with the lack of other plausible suspects and Shingo's own confession, it was getting harder and harder to sustain her belief.

With a sigh, Abigail finished assembling the peanut butter and jelly sandwiches. On a whim, she dug up a few of Grandma's cookie cutters and cut the sandwiches into stars and crescent moons. She piled the shapes on a plate and took them back out to Grandma.

The afternoon was a busy one, but it somehow still managed to drag by. When she locked up behind the last customer, Abigail was fairly certain she never wanted to lay eyes on another tourist again.

"Well," Grandma said as Abigail joined her in the kitchen. "What a perfectly awful day."

"You're telling me. I keep running through all of the facts over and over. What have I missed? What am I not seeing?"

"Maybe we're too close, dear. Maybe we need to put it out of our minds for a bit so we can look at things with fresh eyes. I, for one, know just how I'm going to go about that."

Abigail tilted her head. "What are you going to do?"

"I'm going to cook up a big old elaborate feast. Want to join me?"

"Thanks, Grandma, but I think I might do more harm than good to your feast."

"You're probably right," Grandma agreed. "Though, those peanut butter and jelly sandwiches were charming."

"They better be. They're about the only thing I can cook."

"I wouldn't exactly call that cooking, dear. Why don't you go out for a run?"

"At this time of night?"

"Oh, you know it's not that late. The sun just sets early these days, There's still plenty of light between the street-lamps and the Christmas décor. Go on, honey, the fresh air will do you good."

Abigail gave her shoulders a little shake. Grandma was right. She wasn't doing anybody any good just standing there moping. A jog out in the cold might not solve the case, but it would probably make her feel better.

"Okay, Grandma. I think I'm taking Thor with me. Missy, you wanna come?"

The Shih Tzu popped out of her little bed like a corn

kernel in a hot pan. She dashed out of the kitchen before Grandma or Abigail could say another word.

The night was a clear one. Abigail searched for stars as she stepped off the front porch, but with all of the Christmas lights blazing in the neighborhood, the starlight was drowned out.

The cold air stung her lungs. Her face grew stiff even as her body warmed up to the exercise. Thor ran to and fro on the sidewalk ahead of her, while Missy huffed doggedly at Abigail's side.

She ran until she was exhausted. Poor Missy looked about ready to fall over, and even Thor actually seemed a little winded himself, so Abigail turned and jogged toward home.

It seemed like every house she passed had the window curtains flung wide open. In almost every window was a beautifully decorated Christmas tree. Just beyond the trees, most families seemed to be seated around their dinner tables, eating.

Abigail caught a glimpse of three dark-haired heads clustered together, and for one moment she let herself believe it was the Yamamotos. Then, one of the figures looked out the window and caught sight of her, shattering the little fantasy.

Grandma was still banging around in the kitchen when Abigail made it home again. Missy made a beeline for the kitchen, while Thor simply flopped down in the middle of the floor. Abigail headed upstairs to take a long shower.

She lingered in the steam and heat of the water, but the

delicious smells wafting their way up the stairs soon brought her back down to the kitchen table.

"Any ideas?" Grandma dished pan-fried steak, mashed sweet potatoes, buttered corn, and a piping hot roll onto a plate and set it in front of Abigail.

Abigail picked up a fork and played with her sweet potatoes. "I was hoping you might have one."

Grandma shook her head. "I just keep thinking about Hanako. She is such a bright, cheerful girl. The thought of life dealing her a terrible hand like this is just awful. Taking a parent away... I saw it happen to poor James. I can't stand the thought of it happening again."

Abigail nodded and poked at the food on her plate. It was delicious, and of course it smelled great, but she just didn't really have an appetite.

"Grandma, I've never seen that squirrel nutcracker you always talk about."

"I used to have it on display in the store, but I stopped for two reasons. The first reason was actually Benjamin Guttler. He was such a pest about it all those years ago, he single-handedly persuaded me to keep my Shingo collection to myself."

"What's the second reason?"

"Shingo asked me not to."

"*Shingo* did?"

"He's embarrassed by the craftsmanship. Silly, don't you think? He made it as a young teen. There's nothing to be embarrassed about."

"Can I see it?"

"Of course you can, dear. It's somewhere in the attic."

Abigail pushed her plate back. "Dinner was delicious, but I just can't seem to work up an appetite. I'm sorry."

"Don't be." Grandma sighed, pushing back her own plate. "I'm not really hungry either. I'll pack everything up, and we can have it for lunch or dinner tomorrow. We won't waste a morsel. Maybe we can even take some of it to Madeline and Hanako."

Abigail stood. "I'm going to hunt around the attic for the squirrel."

"Sure thing. Just keep an eye out for ghosts." Grandma winked.

"Come on, Grandma. I've been up in that attic before. It's spooky, but nothing… supernatural… I don't think."

Grandma shrugged. "If you say so. But you've never come back down without a whiff of the past still clinging to your clothes."

CHAPTER TWENTY-FOUR

Climbing up into the attic was like climbing into a black hole.

The cold pricked Abigail's cheeks, while the stale, dusty air crept up her nose and triggered a sneeze. When she went to cover her mouth with the crook of her elbow, she realized she couldn't see past her forearm; her hand had been swallowed by the darkness.

Shivering, Abigail hurried to find the switch that would light the single bare bulb. She had to step out of the glow splashing in from below the spiral staircase, and for a terrifying second, she felt blind. Then, her hands found the switch, and the room was bathed in a warm orange-tinged light.

She let out a breath and chuckled to herself. Grandma mentioning ghosts must've really gotten to her.

"If I were a squirrel, where would I be?" Her words bounced back at her, hard and hollow.

The attic was a tidy one, as far as attics went. Almost everything was put up in neatly stacked boxes which hugged the corners of the room, leaving the middle of the floor bare. The real problem was that none of the boxes were reliably marked. In fact, only one box displayed any writing, and that was a single unhelpful word: Egg.

Abigail shrugged and started in on the nearest corner. She made it all the way to the third corner of the room before finding a small chest inside a standard box. The chest was made of polished wood, and when she lifted the lid, the fragrance of cedar puffed up from the crushed tissue paper.

She found it.

The squirrel was surprisingly simple. Nothing like the phoenix she'd seen at the toy store. It was heavy, and the wood grain glowed red and bright. In Abigail's hands, it felt quite light for its size.

She pulled the squirrel from its home and peered at it closely. It was made up of at least three pieces: the head, the front of the body with little movable arms, and the back with a movable tail.

At the bottom, just underneath the tail, was a little crank. Abigail turned the crank and watched the tail flick suddenly. Next, the squirrel turned its head from side to side, as if looking around to make sure the coast was clear. Finally, its mouth popped open just as its hands swung up with tremendous force, stopping a fraction below the squirrel's thick front teeth.

Smiling, Abigail began to crank again when she realized her index finger lay on something especially cold. Flipping the squirrel over, she turned toward the light and gasped.

"Grandma!" she shouted and hurried out of the cold, creepy attic. "Grandma!"

"Abigail? Are you all right?"

She followed the sound of Grandma's voice down the hall and found her grandmother in a nightgown, clutching Missy for dear life.

"What is it? You scared me half to death!"

"Sorry, Grandma, but take a look at this."

Seeing the squirrel, Grandma broke into a fond grin. "You found it! Isn't he handsome?"

"It's gorgeous, but look at that crank."

Grandma tuned the automaton over and peered at the crank before her eyes grew suddenly wide. "A metal screw!"

"I almost didn't notice it; I was so distracted by its movements."

"Well, isn't that peculiar?"

"I know he prides himself on never using any material outside of wood and springs, but maybe his older designs were cruder."

Grandma frowned. "Come in here a minute, Abigail."

She followed her grandmother into the master bedroom and over to a slender curio cabinet that seemed to be made entirely of gold and glass. Inside were more shelves than Abigail had ever seen in a curio before.

"Wow, Grandma, where did this come from?"

"Oh, this old thing?" Grandma said with a sly smile. "This piece was certainly an adventure to get my hands on. I'll tell you about it some other time. Right now, help me look through these Shingo originals."

The curio was full of wooden automata. They sat neatly in clusters and rows, like steadfast soldiers in an otherworldly army.

"I keep them all arranged in order of creation. This little guy belongs on the top shelf, right between the miniature swan and the archer." Grandma set the squirrel in its rightful place.

Abigail picked up the archer and turned it delicately over in her hands. "He has a screw too! Right here! A tiny one."

"Wait a minute," Grandma said, squinting at the third shelf. "Look here. This is the first in his signature series. It doesn't have any screws, but the one just before it does. He must have stopped using screws here."

Abigail frowned. "What was so special about the signature series? Why stop using screws then?"

"Let me see. His signature series were the first designs he started selling commercially. He released these when he first opened up his shop after college."

Abigail felt a little pop in her head. "Grandma, that's it."

"What?"

"I think I know what happened."

CHAPTER TWENTY-FIVE

Early the next morning, before the police station was even open, Abigail, Grandma, and Madeline stood shivering at the front door.

"Willy will be here any second," Grandma said through chattering teeth.

"Think he'll be happy to see us?"

"No. Well, yes, but he won't admit it. He'll grumble and fuss and remind us he's the sheriff. Whatever he says, don't back down, Madeline."

Madeline said nothing, but she nodded her pale face once, and her eyes took on a hard, determined edge.

It was so early, and the weather was so cold, that the streets of Wallace Point were finally empty of tourists. The only people out and about were locals walking their dogs or jogging. So when the long white car marked "Sheriff" pulled into the small parking lot next to the station, the trio of women immediately stiffened their spines.

"Here we go, girls," Grandma muttered, as Sheriff William Wilson walked toward them. "Good morning, Willy!"

The sheriff glared at Abigail, nodded deferentially to Madeline, and avoided Grandma's eyes altogether. Without a word, he began fishing through his ring of keys.

"Now, Willy," Grandma admonished. "Don't be rude."

"What is it, Florence?"

"Oh, Willy," Grandma began, but Sheriff Wilson cut her off.

"Don't 'oh, Willy' me, Florence. Not this time. I've got to get inside and get to work. I'm the sheriff, after all. The man has confessed. It pains me just as much as it pains you, but that's the reality." He groaned as the keyring slipped from his slightly trembling hands and clattered down onto the concrete sidewalk.

Madeline Yamamoto knelt gracefully, picked up the keys with her pale, steady hands, and handed them back to Willy. "I want to speak with Shingo."

The sheriff searched Madeline's face, and for a moment, Abigail saw the older man's shoulders slump. But then he glanced at Abigail and at Grandma before meeting Madeline's gaze again.

"No," he said simply.

"Willy!" Grandma snapped.

"Good morning, Sheriff!" called a cheery voice from the parking lot. Abigail whirled around. She'd definitely heard that voice before.

It took her a second to place Officer Reynolds's face. So much had happened since she confronted him at the pier about the missing evidence, that she had almost forgotten about him. It took him longer to recognize her, but when he did, his anxiety was unmistakable.

"How can I h-help—" The officer's face flushed red, and he actually choked on his words. Coughing hard, he bent over and put his hands on his knees as he tried to suck in air.

"Are you all right, son?" the sheriff asked, genuinely concerned.

Abigail moved to Officer Reynolds's side and thumped him hard on the back twice. "There, there, officer. Is that better?"

Officer Reynolds nodded and quickly sidestepped away from Abigail and closer to Sheriff Wilson. "What's going on here?"

"Our two favorite amateur detectives want to talk to our suspect," Sheriff Wilson snorted. "But I'd rather they not. This case is muddy enough as it is."

The corners of Officer Reynolds's mouth twitched. Abigail had no idea what the guy was thinking, but she knew she didn't trust him for a moment.

"Say, Officer Reynolds," she said quickly. "Don't I know you from somewhere? You seem awfully familiar."

Sheriff Wilson rolled his eyes. "Officer Reynolds has been

a respected member of the police force for a couple years now, Abigail. You've probably seen him around town. Now, if you ladies will please excuse us, we have real work to do. Reynolds? Have you got a key? My fingers aren't cooperating in this cold."

Officer Reynolds nodded and stepped toward the door. As he fished in his pockets for his keys, Abigail noticed a sheen of sweat forming on his forehead.

Madeline took a step closer to Sheriff Wilson. "Sheriff, I apologize for what my Shingo has put you through. I know you must be tired of this case and all the confusion surrounding it." She kept her eyes down, and her head slightly bowed. "I am ashamed that my family has caused all this trouble. But he is my husband, and I know deep down he's a good man. Please don't keep me away from him. Please let Florence and Abigail help me."

Officer Reynolds unlocked the door and slipped in to shut off the alarm. Without a second's hesitation, Grandma slipped in right behind him.

"Florence!" Sheriff Wilson moaned, but Abigail was already darting in behind Grandma.

"You're not going to keep three women out in the cold, are you Willy?" Grandma tutted.

Sheriff Wilson sighed as he held the door open for Madeline and followed them inside.

"Let 'em talk to him, Sheriff," Officer Reynolds said quietly. He had turned off the alarm and stood with his back against the wall. His eyes flicked toward Abigail before focusing on his boss again. "What harm could it do?"

Sheriff Wilson frowned at his officer. "Nice job having my back, Reynolds." Despite his words, his voice had lost its obstinate tone. Shrugging a shoulder, he turned to Grandma. "Make it quick, Florence. Shingo's been practically catatonic, so don't do anything to make him any worse."

Grandma's lower lip jutted out at him. "Why do you always doubt me, Willy?"

"Yeah, I don't know," the sheriff said, throwing up his hands. "I just wish you'd let me solve a case for once!"

"Thank you, Sheriff," Madeline said quietly.

The sheriff nodded and left the room.

Officer Reynolds waved them over. "Come with me. I'll show you to the interrogation room while the sheriff gets Shingo ready."

Officer Reynolds brought an extra chair into the interrogation room, which was cold and bare, save for a single table. The women settled themselves into the seats and waited.

Soon, Sheriff Wilson led Shingo in. Abigail almost gasped at the change in Shingo. At the grand reopening of his toy store, his eyes sparkled with intelligence and curiosity. His demeanor, though quiet, had been confident and poised.

Now, he looked as if he'd aged ten years. His shoulders stooped, his eyes were dull and listless, and his feet dragged along the floor.

Sheriff Wilson got Shingo into a chair and secured his

hands and feet, then, arching an eyebrow at Grandma, he left the room.

Abigail looked at Grandma, who smiled at her encouragingly. Then, Abigail looked at Madeline. Her eyes were filled with tears and pain, but her face remained calm. The woman took a deep, silent breath before nodding at Abigail.

Abigail pulled her chair closer to Shingo and said in the calmest, most soothing voice she could manage, "I know you didn't do it, Shingo."

He didn't respond. His eyes stayed on the table, and even his breathing remained shallow.

"I know you didn't do it, but I know you do blame yourself."

He looked up at her then, and Abigail caught a spark of the man she had met before.

"You made that toy cannon, the one that killed Dallas. You made it years ago while you were still in college. Back then, Dallas abused your trust. You took him under your wing, and yet he turned on you. He harassed you, provoked you. He dug through your trash like an animal. When all that wasn't enough, he went after Madeline. He thought he could charm her away from you and cause you even more pain.

"But when Madeline rejected his advances, he became even more desperate. He broke into your room, and the university didn't do a thing about it. Dallas was too rich, too well-connected for the college to touch.

"That was when you began to consider taking drastic action. You weren't sleeping. You alienated Madeline and those who cared about you. He even broke into your room, which made you understandably paranoid. So, you used your skills against him. You created a weapon that could protect you when no one else would.

"That's why the automaton had screws. You made it while you were still learning, before you'd honed the skills you have now. You made it years ago, but you never used it. In fact, you threw it out."

Shingo looked away. "I never should have made it."

"But that's the important thing: You realized in time that you were taking things too far. You realized you weren't a murderer. You did the right thing. But Dallas hadn't stopped digging through your trash. He found the automaton and quickly realized what it was for. Thinking that you still wanted to kill him, he transferred schools."

Shingo blinked. "So that's why he finally left me alone?"

"At least for a little while. But without your designs to steal, Dallas just couldn't cut it. He never did anything big or innovative. He did so little that even a thorough background check didn't turn anything up on the guy.

"Now that he was struggling to make ends meet, his thoughts returned to you. If only you continued to teach him despite his harassment of you. In his eyes, it was all your fault.

"So he looked you up. He saw how successful you were, how truly genius your creations were, and his old grudge flared back up again. He wanted to right the wrongs he thought you had done to him. And what better way than to use your own automata against you on the night of your grand reopening?"

"To be so obsessed with me..." Shingo shook his head. "I don't understand. I'm just a craftsman."

"Dallas was obsessed with your happiness, because all he had was envy and bitterness. So he came to the reopening. While Hanako, Grandma, and I were in the opposite room, he used the crowd of tourists and collectors as cover while he slipped into the back hall and found the locked room.

"He broke in, locked himself in from the inside, and began to set up the trap. But he wasn't as clever as he should have been. The cannon went off, and he took it point blank in the gut. It took the Sheriff so long to get inside the room that Dallas knew he was a goner.

"So he used the last weapon he had available: his own death. With his last breath, he told the sheriff that this was all your doing. But it wasn't. His selfish obsession did this to him."

Slowly, Shingo nodded, and Madeline let out a deep, rushing sigh. When he spoke, Shingo looked only at his wife.

"I am ashamed to have ever considered killing Dallas. He was insufferable, but he was still a human being, a human being who was in pain and turmoil, and the only way he knew how to deal with it was by taking it out on me."

Abigail insisted, "That doesn't make you responsible for his death. Not in the slightest."

"But I made that cannon that killed him. And maybe if I

had treated him with more kindness, maybe if I had been more understanding..."

Grandma leaned forward then. She waited until Shingo met her eyes, and then she said very seriously, "You are not responsible for his actions, Shingo. For some people, it's never enough. Their selfishness is a black hole that can never be satiated."

Shingo looked away, his expression unconvinced.

Grandma continued, "I know it's hard to believe that. I had a hard time believing I wasn't responsible for how Sarah turned out or for how my marriage fell apart. But Sarah made her own choices, and so did my husband. And so did I."

Grandma's voice broke a little, but she cleared her throat and pushed on. "You owed him nothing. You cannot blame yourself for any of this. You may have made the gun, but he's the one who pulled the trigger. The people you do owe are Madeline and Hanako, who have always supported you, and who need you now more than ever. You must not take the blame for this, for their sake."

Madeline reached out her hand and set it atop of Shingo's. She looked at him steadily, but her voice shook as she spoke. "Shingo, my love, is somebody as selfish as Dallas worth throwing away your life? Is he worth throwing Hanako away? Is he worth throwing me away?"

Finally, Shingo's eyes filled with tears. He began to rock back and forth in his seat until, breaking down, he rested his forehead against the cold table and began to sob quietly. "All right," he murmured. "I'll talk to Sheriff Wilson. I'll make this right."

Grandma stood up, and Abigail followed her lead. Pausing briefly at the door, they saw Madeline wrap her arms around her husband's shoulders and bury her head inside the crook of his neck.

CHAPTER TWENTY-SIX

I t was the week before Christmas, and Wallace Point could hardly contain all of its winter cheer. Abigail couldn't believe her eyes when she took her morning run.

"Grandma," she called, trotting into the store with Thor. "I didn't think it could happen, but it did."

"In here, dear." Grandma's voice floated into the store from the living room. Abigail found her curled up on the couch with Missy, who had decided to be bad and skip her usual workout. Grandma put the morning paper down and smiled at Abigail. "What were you saying?"

"The neighborhood is getting even more Christmasy. I actually saw people putting up more lights and décor. I swear I even saw someone with a snow machine, adding more snow to their yard."

"Well, what do you expect? Wallace Point has a reputation to uphold. By the way, have I mentioned we're closing the shop early today?"

"No. Why?"

"Tonight is the annual Christmas tree lighting."

"Do you really need a Christmas tree when you already have a papier-mâché cow hoisted up on the roof of a church?"

"That's a silly question. The event starts just before sunset, so we won't reopen after lunch."

Abigail shrugged. "That's fine by me. I'm going to head upstairs and shower."

"All right dear. I think I might start on breakfast."

Abigail didn't linger under the hot water that morning. Closing the store early made her feel like a kid skipping school: slightly guilty, yet mostly thrilled.

The most recent developments in the Yamamoto case were also boosting her mood. After Shingo finally told Willy Wilson the truth, the old sheriff had launched a full-fledged investigation into Dallas Redford.

Sheriff Wilson had contacted detectives in Dallas's hometown. A thorough search of his house had produced plenty of evidence to support Shingo's story. Perhaps the most critical piece of evidence was on Dallas's personal computer.

He'd written hundreds of emails to Shingo, emails he never sent. All the emails were threatening, talking about ways that Dallas would make Shingo pay for ruining his life. One email went on for paragraphs about how Dallas had learned to lock pick, ending with the threat, "You'll never be able to lock me out again." Several of the emails even boasted about Dallas owning the deadly cannon.

Abigail had felt totally disgusted with Dallas. His cowardice not only cost him his life, but it almost robbed a wife of her husband, and a child of her father.

But as Grandma had said, "That is all in the past. In the present, everything is just the way it should be."

THAT AFTERNOON, Grandma and Abigail walked quickly, trying to keep warm by staying in motion. They weren't the only ones. The sidewalks swarmed with tourists and residents alike, all of them heading in the same direction.

"Is there anything special about this tree, Grandma? Did pirates plant it the night of the hoisting?"

Grandma laughed. "No, but they may as well have. This tree is over three hundred years old, and it's still going strong."

The crowd pushed and jostled them along until they joined a mass of bodies surrounding a large oak. Its branches were so thick and heavy that some of them actually dipped into the earth for extra support before swinging back up toward the sky. Though it had lost its leaves for the winter, the strong, reaching arms still made the tree look regal and proud.

"Do you have your ornament?" Grandma asked. Her cheeks looked like two plump red apples.

"Yep."

"Let's push our way through, then. We need to hang them before they light the tree."

Grandma began to elbow her way through the crowd, Abigail following close behind. A couple of people opened their mouths to complain, but as soon as they saw little Florence Lane smiling sweetly up at them, their mouths snapped shut. Abigail laughed under her breath; the gaping tourists reminded her of Shingo's squirrel nutcracker.

The tree was already embellished with the ornaments from most of Wallace Point's residents. Tourists were adding their own baubles and decorations too. Grandma and Abigail added their trinkets to a low hanging branch.

"All right, now we have to step back a bit."

"Why? We have front row seats, Grandma."

"Front row seats won't do it. When this big old tree lights up, you have to stand pretty far away to appreciate it."

Grandma led her back through the crowd, and Abigail caught sight of a few friends. Sally and her father, Bobby Kent, stood side by side. His megawatt smile flashed at anyone who glanced his way. Camille Bellerose and Piper Fischer seemed to be politely listening to a teenager Abigail had never seen before. Kirby Madsen stood with his arms crossed, frowning mightily while a pretty young tourist attempted to flirt with Dag. Lanky Lee stood with the

Madsen brothers. His arms were crossed too, but he looked like a string bean next to the Viking descendants.

Finally, Grandma found a suitable place in the crowd and stopped. Just as they were turning around to face the tree, Abigail caught sight of the Yamamotos.

"Look, Grandma. It's Shingo and his family. Oh, and Yuri too!"

"Really? Where?"

Abigail jerked her head toward the family. Grandma found the little group in the crowd and arched her eyebrows. "Goodness. I'm dying to know that story."

A tourist behind them said in wonderment, "Look, they're starting."

Abigail and Grandma turned their attention back to the tree. A microphone crackled to life and someone—Abigail couldn't see who, thanks to the crowd—gave a brief history of the annual lighting. Then, as the sun fully set and dusk enveloped the crowd, the countdown began. "Ten!" started the speaker alone, and by the time he reached "one" the entire crowd had joined in, letting out huge cheers as the lights on the tree blinked on.

Every naked branch, every bare limb of the tree had been swathed in tiny lights. On the topmost boughs, the Christmas lights seemed to almost join the stars.

"Wow, Grandma, that's beautiful."

"Yes," Grandma agreed. "Good old Wallace Point."

Unfortunately, the tourists were impatient. As soon as the tree was lit and the round of applause died down, they began to mill back toward downtown. The locals, however, moved in the opposite direction to gather under the tree.

Grandma grabbed Abigail's hand. "Come on. Let's go say hello to the Yamamotos."

Hanako caught sight of them first. "Granny Lane!" she cried out, throwing her arms around Grandma's waist. "When are you going to bring me more cookies?"

"Hanako!" admonished Madeline, but Grandma just threw her head back and laughed.

"I think I can squeeze in one more delivery before Christmas."

"That is very kind of you, Granny Lane," Shingo said. Abigail was happy to notice that he stood straight and tall again, and that his eyes had regained their bright look of confidence and intelligence.

"I think, though, that we should be the ones baking cookies for *you*," Madeline chimed in. "Thank you again, both of you, for all of your help."

"We're just happy things worked out in the end," Abigail said, watching Hanako's smiling face.

Grandma nodded. "That's right. Now, I would love to meet your guest." She motioned at Yuri.

"Excuse us," Madeline blushed. "Florence and Abigail, this is Yuri, Shingo's cousin."

Yuri stepped forward to extend her hand, but her eyes narrowed. "Actually, I think we've met before, back at Kirby's bar."

"Nonsense. That didn't count. We were never properly

introduced. It's a pleasure to officially meet you." Grandma took Yuri's hand and gave it a firm shake.

Shingo asked, "You've met my cousin before?"

Yuri laughed as she recalled, "More or less. They accosted me while I was drowning my sorrows with—err—" Yuri glanced at Hanako, who was staring up at her intently. "Soda. I was drowning my sorrows with soda."

"Soda is bad for you, Auntie Yuri."

"Thank you, Hanako. I'll try to remember that next time."

Abigail admitted, her cheeks flushing red, "Honestly, I thought maybe you had something to do with the whole fiasco."

Yuri blinked. "Really? What about me gives you the killer vibes?"

"At the grand reopening, you were acting very odd. You kept looking around as if you were looking for someone or were afraid of getting caught. That, and you had something big with you, something you tried to hide under your coat."

For a second, Yuri's face darkened. "That was supposed to be a surprise."

"Oh?"

"It was a gift. I was going to give it to Shingo tonight, in fact."

Abigail snapped her mouth shut. "Oh! I hope I didn't ruin the surprise."

Madeline smiled. "Of course not. We were going to open the gifts at home after the tree lighting ceremony. Actually, why don't you two stop by?"

Abigail looked over at Grandma. "That would be lovely, don't you think, Grandma?"

Grandma smiled. "What should we bring?"

Shingo shook his head and squeezed Grandma's hand. "You've done so much for us. Think of yourselves as our Christmas gift."

CHAPTER TWENTY-SEVEN

G randma and Abigail showed up at the Yamamoto
house with a tin of cookies and a wrapped Christmas
gift.

Madeline greeted them with a big hug before taking their
coats and leading them to the living room.

Abigail and Grandma looked around, their faces filled
with wonderment. They saw strings of amber lights
adorning the fireplace and windows. A Christmas tree,
covered with gold glass balls and handmade ornaments, sat
in one corner with a dozen gifts laying at its base. Soft
seasonal music played throughout the house, while the smell
of incense infused the air.

"Oh my goodness!" Grandma said.

Abigail shared her sentiment. "Wow, you guys really went
all out!" She walked over to the mantel and lightly touched

the small automaton of a Santa reading a children's book to youngsters gathered around his feet. Every now and then, the Santa would lower his book in one hand, then hold his belly with the other, and drop his head back in a laugh. The children at his feet moved back and forth, as if laughing too.

"Here, Granny Lane, let me help you," Madeline said as she escorted Grandma to a seat at their high back sofa.

"Thank you, dear," Grandma replied while handing her the tin of cookies.

"Look, Hanako!" Madeline said. "Granny Lane's famous cookies!" Her daughter promptly plopped beside Grandma.

"Thank you, Granny!" Hanako gave Grandma a hug.

"My pleasure, darling. Oh, and my granddaughter has something special for your family. Abigail?"

Abigail turned from the mantel, still holding the wrapped gift. "Ah, yes. Grandma found something perfect for you guys at the shop." She walked over to the armchair where Shingo sat and handed him the wrapped box.

"Oh, you two have done so much for me already," Shingo said. Regardless, soon the paper was off and neatly piled on the floor beside him, and he carefully opened the box. He removed the tissue paper and slowly raised a large snow globe of a family of three wearing winter jackets, standing hand-in-hand by a decorated Christmas tree. Smiles were painted on their faces in great detail.

"There's a switch at the bottom," Abigail said as she joined Grandma at the sofa.

"Ooh, push it!" Hanako exclaimed.

Shingo turned it upside down, flipped the switch, then turned it back to reveal that the tree was lit up with small lights.

Shingo's face lit up. "This is so beautiful! Thank you." He turned to his daughter. "Hanako, please place this carefully on the mantel beside the Santa display."

With the globe in hand, Hanako headed over to the mantel with measured steps, her velvety green Christmas dress swishing with every movement.

After she placed the globe gently beside the Santa display, she turned and announced, "My turn!" She ran over to the Christmas tree, picked up a round hat box, then returned to her father.

"Papa, here's your catnip!" she said as she carefully placed the hat box in his lap. "Open it!"

Her dad laughed while shaking his head quizzically. "What do you mean by 'catnip,' dear? We don't own a cat."

Hanako took a deep, serious breath, then explained, "Granny Lane is always trying to figure out the one thing each of her customers can't resist. Sometimes it's old books, ships, ponies… but whatever it is, that's the person's catnip, and she finds an antique that matches!"

"So," he began, "catnip is something unique to an individual that they enjoy or collect?"

Abigail nodded. "Correct. It's finding the perfect gift that shows the person receiving it that you get them, and you appreciate them." She looked at Grandma, who winked back at her.

"Well, c'mon, Papa! Open it already!"

Shingo opened the lid to the hat box and carefully took out a wooden automaton of a slender male figure brandishing a tool: a toy maker, just like him! He turned it on to see the figure had a lighted magnifying glass hanging out on a pivoted metal arm in front of his face.

He turned his head toward his daughter and smiled widely. "It's exquisite!"

"It's your catnip, isn't it?" she asked as her wide eyes looked at him.

"It is, indeed."

"I ended up borrowing some of your supplies to make it. I hope that's okay."

Shingo wiped a tear from his eye and placed the automaton back into the hat box. "It's more than all right. Come give me a hug." He stretched out his arms to Hanako and pulled her in tight.

She squeezed him back with all of her might.

Yuri, who had been sitting very quietly on the love seat, gave a little sniffle.

Grandma looked around the room. "It would appear, there isn't a dry eye in the house." She laughed.

Abigail had to admit, she was a little teary-eyed too. But she did her best to hide it. "So, Yuri. How come you and Shingo lost touch?"

Yuri cast a look at Shingo, who smiled at her encouragingly. "That's kind of a long story," she began. "When Shingo and I were much younger, we used to be very close. But I started getting jealous of all the attention he was getting for his automata. And he stopped hanging out with me too, since he was always working on those things.

"So I broke one he was in the middle of building. He caught me, and we never talked again after that. I kept the broken automaton all these years. This year, I fixed it and completed it myself, and I was going to give it to him as a Christmas gift and a peace offering. But then... well, the gunshot went off and I never had the chance."

Shingo put his arm firmly around his cousin's shoulders. "We have a chance now. That's what's important."

Yuri stood up, walked over to the tree, and bent down to retrieve a gift bag. "Anyhow, I believe this is yours." She walked over to him and kissed his cheek before handing the gift bag to Shingo.

He smiled up at her and reached into the bag, taking out an intricate wooden squirrel.

Grandma gasped. "That looks like a squirrel he gave me many years ago."

Hanako asked, "Was he my age?"

"Hmm." Grandma touched her chin, as if in deep thought. "I believe he was fifteen."

"Dang, and I'm only eight!"

Shingo ruffled his daughter's hair. "You go easy on your old man. I wasn't a savant like you." He then turned to his cousin. "Yuri, I'm so sorry too. All the years we missed!"

Yuri smiled and leaned in to whisper something to him.

"My goodness! Where are my manners?" Shingo walked

over to the tree and picked up a large gift bag, bringing it over to Grandma. "I believe I may have found your 'catnip.' Tell me if I'm right."

Grandma wasn't shy about digging into the gift bag, and in moments she pulled out her gift. "Oh, goodness! An antique Polaroid Land camera!" The collapsible camera had leather accents, a matching case, and miscellaneous accessories. "I've never seen one in such perfect condition. Abigail, watch." Grandma expanded the camera, then collapsed it again.

"Won't James be jealous?" Abigail commented. "It looks like something a spy would have!"

Shingo nodded at the gift bag. "There's more. Keep digging."

Grandma pulled out a new box of film. "They still make these?"

"They just started reproducing the film again."

"Oh, looks like there's more..." Grandma pulled out a small photo album, with slots sized for Polaroid film. "Oh, how wonderful!"

"I want you two to fill that album with your own memories together. Live your life together as if you never spent it apart."

Granny Lane wiped more tears from her eyes. "Thank you. That was so thoughtful... Now, help this old lady up so we can all take a bunch of pictures to fill our album together!"

BACK HOME, Abigail decided to take Thor out for a walk before holing up for the evening. They set out at a brisk pace, trying once again to beat the weather. The sky was overcast so she couldn't see the stars. But the general Christmas décor was plenty to light her way.

"So, Thor," she said conversationally. The Great Dane wagged his tail and looked up at her, giving her his undivided attention. "All of this mushy Christmas stuff has me thinking I should call Mom."

Thor sneezed.

"I know what you're thinking. But, you know, maybe Mom could finally let go of whatever grudge she feels she has against Grandma. She could come spend Christmas with us. Grandma can bake cookies, and—"

Thor sneezed again. This time, he added a little whine.

Abigail sighed. "You're right. That's a horrible idea. I just still haven't thought of a good Christmas gift for Grandma. I've been racking my brain, but what do you give someone who's already so pleased with life?"

"Abigail? Are you all right?"

Abigail's head jerked up. In her heart-to-heart with Thor, she hadn't paid much attention to where her feet were taking her. She saw now that she had found her way to Camille's house. The woman was in her garden again.

"Camille, you scared me!"

"Well, you scared me first. Who were you talking to?"

"Thor."

"Ah. How's that going?"

"Well, he has good instincts, but he's not great at communicating his ideas."

"Maybe I could help?"

"I'm just trying to think of something special to get or do for Grandma for Christmas. I just can't come up with any good ideas."

"She does a lot of cooking and baking for other people… Maybe you could make a whole meal for her. And I think there's been a bit of tension between her and Willy over the Yamamoto case, hasn't there? Maybe you could invite him. Let them clear the air. Oh, and you could invite James too. It's Christmas after all. It'd be such a lovely gathering."

Abigail blinked. "Camille, you just solved all my problems in one fell swoop."

"What can I say?" Camille said, grinning. "I'm a teacher."

CHAPTER TWENTY-EIGHT

The rolls refused to rise. The cheese sauce for the baked macaroni tasted bland. The potatoes wouldn't mash, and the ham smelled like it was burning after only fifteen minutes in the oven.

Abigail looked around her at the mess in the kitchen. She had an hour before she was supposed to unveil her big surprise to Grandma, and her meal was a disaster.

"Camille!" she growled, panic rising in her throat. "I can't believe I let you talk me into thinking I could actually cook a whole meal by myself."

"Cupcake?"

Abigail whirled around. James stood in the doorway, his eyebrows arched at the piles of mixing bowls and food scraps scattered around the kitchen. "Who were you talking to?"

"Camille. What are you doing here? You're early."

Like a thief caught red-handed, James threw his palms up and backed up against the wall. "I figured you could use some help, so I came over early. Apparently, I was right."

Abigail flopped into one of the chairs at the little kitchen table. As she did, a cloud of flour puffed up from her shirt. "I'm more of a microwave-meals kind of gal."

"Me too, minus the gal part." James dropped his hands. He took a step forward and crouched in front of Abigail so they were at eye-level. "But it doesn't take a master chef to know that doubling the oven temperature won't halve the cooking time."

"It makes sense, though!"

James laughed as he lowered the oven temperature. "The world of cooking defies the normal laws of nature. Where's Granny Lane?"

"She's upstairs. She promised not to come down until six."

"Great. What do you say we get this place cleaned up?"

Really, Abigail did the cleaning up while James took over the cooking. He added more seasoning to the mac and cheese and popped the dish into the oven. He covered the ham with aluminum foil to prevent any further blackening. He even managed to smooth out the mashed potatoes, though the rolls were a complete loss.

The whole time he worked, he whistled Christmas tunes one after another, like an overzealous songbird.

"You seem to be in a good mood." Abigail wiped the last fleck of butter off the table.

"I am. You remember Officer Reynolds?"

Abigail's knee jerked and hit the underside of the wooden table. James glanced at her.

"Ha, clumsy me! Um, yeah, I think I remember Officer Reynolds. He, uh, helped persuade your father to let us see Shingo. Besides that, I've never interacted with him in any other capacity."

James eyed her suspiciously. "Well, he came up to me out of the blue and offered to help me with the cold Ripper cases."

"Wow," Abigail said, more to herself than to James. She honestly didn't think Officer Reynolds would consider her suggestion to help out James. "He's actually doing it."

"What was that?"

"I said, you're actually doing it. You're digging back into the Ripper case."

"Yeah. Who knows if I'll turn anything up, but I do feel like I need to try."

"Speaking of mysteries, whatever happened with the sock monkey case?"

James grinned. "I'm so glad you asked. I found the culprit! But the information I'm about to give you is confidential."

"Okay, but can I tell Grandma?"

"Well, she's in the Granny Gang, so she either already knows, or will know soon enough. But don't tell anyone else. Not even my father."

"Of course," Abigail promised, though she couldn't understand what was so dire about the case's solution.

James leaned in close. "The sock monkey maker is none other than our town's dark and mysterious Kirby."

Abigail's mouth dropped open. "No way!"

"Yup. I happened to be at the bowling alley when I saw him give one to a child. I cornered him and asked him what gives, and then he confessed. For a brick wall of a man, he crumbled pretty easily once I laid on the pressure. Poor guy seemed so embarrassed."

"He shouldn't be. He's got amazing skills!"

"That's what I told him. I explained that the Granny Gang hired me to find the monkey-making culprit, that they weren't happy about the competition."

"Why would he pick making sock monkeys of all hobbies?"

"He told me he used to whittle his time away tying various sailor knots into rope. He knows them all and likes to practice, something his dad taught him when he was younger. But that got boring, so he took up sewing. Then one day he stumbled upon a how-to sock monkey book and realized he could take his sewing to the next level."

"So now the Granny Gang knows?"

"Not only do they know, but they've also made him a secret honorary member of the gang. He wasn't exactly eager to be a member, but he was given a choice: join, or be outed to the whole town. He's got a macho reputation to uphold, so he gave in to their demands. Now he's gotta supply at least one monkey a week to the gang's stash."

"Man, this town and its secrets! Now I have another one to keep!"

James chuckled.

A knock sounded at the front of the store. When Abigail answered it, Sheriff Wilson stood there with two bouquets of roses in his hands and a sheepish smile on his face.

"Hello, Abigail, thank you for the invitation." He thrust a bouquet into her hands. The roses in this bouquet were a soft pink with bits of white just at the tips.

"Thank you, Willy. You didn't have to bring anything."

"Oh, yes I did. I've been pushing Florence's buttons ever since I had to take in Shingo."

"Well, come on in. I was just about to let Grandma come back down."

Abigail ran upstairs and tapped on Grandma's door. "Grandma, we're ready for you!"

Grandma's white-haired head popped out of the door. "We? Who's *we*?"

"Come down and see."

Abigail linked her arm through Grandma's and helped her down the stairs.

"Oh! What are those delicious smells?" She stopped short. "Abigail, you put together a meal?"

"I tried," Abigail admitted. "It's actually all edible. I tried a little bit of everything to be sure."

Grandma looked relieved, though to her credit, she did try to hide it.

James and Willy waited in the living room next to the fire. When Grandma turned the corner, she gasped at her surprise guests. The sheriff walked up to Grandma and offered her the bouquet. These roses were a deep red, and all of the blooms had fully opened.

Grandma's eyes filled with tears. "Oh, my! I couldn't be any luckier, could I? I get to spend my Christmas with my favorite two young men and my darling granddaughter."

Willy blushed and scuffed his shoe against the ornate rug. "I wouldn't call me young, Florence."

Grandma brought her nose to the bouquet and inhaled deeply. When she spoke again, her eyes were sparkling. "You're looking younger than ever to me."

She offered her arm, and Willy took it. He led her to the kitchen, his face both red and radiant. With a grin, James bowed and offered Abigail his arm, which she accepted after dramatically rolling her eyes.

Only Thor and Missy remained in the living room before the fire. Thor sidled over to the smaller dog and nudged her belly. She licked his nose, then the two trotted past the Christmas tree, all lit up with lights, and followed their family into the kitchen.

ABOUT THE AUTHOR

Mysteries run in the family, starting all the way back to my great grandmother. I grew up watching old black and white movies like The Thin Man and Rebecca, and reading classic mysteries by Poe, Doyle, and Christie.

Outside of writing mysteries, I love old steamships, 1990s adventure puzzle games, and trusty pets. I live in a coastal New England town with my hideous (yet charming) Chihuahua, Fugly.